Arcadium Autum Emporium
TALES OF THE GATEKEEPER

Arcadium Autum Emporium
TALES OF THE GATEKEEPER

BY

M. Kari Barr

HeartString Publishing

HeartString Publishing
a Division of Stone Creek Farms
P.O. Box 734
Airway Heights WA 99022

Because I can . . .

Special thanks to my writing and critique groups.
Namely, Not Your Mother's Writing Group,

The Wednesday Writers, and Spokane Fiction Writers.

The help I have received has kept my stories from embarrassing me too much. That's a good thing.

Prologue

Being that I guard the way, they call me the gatekeeper. As for me, I prefer Portal Master. The job itself is not entirely as glamorous as all that. . . okay, not glamorous at all.

What I do is sit in this dim Arcadium. A gallery dedicated to the strange and arcane. I collect and sometimes sell these artifacts, whimsies collected over the centuries. Items like Scindalian's Sword or (purportedly) a snippet of Horvath's Beard. Bottles and bottles of Fairy Dust, of course, tis easy to collect Dust, heh heh.

By far, my most valued collection is, of course, the stories. Of course, of course...I will say it as many times as I like. Don't mind me, I'm not a grammarian. I am the touted lover of books.

And just how do I collect said tales, you might ask? Ah, now those explanations are as varied as the tales themselves. But, truly for the most part, I gather them through extortion.

Ah, now put away your judgment. Tis no crime. My king sent me here ages ago to guard the portal. Whether it was a punishment or out of pity I know not. Either way, here I am, trapped inside this existence, unable to leave. Though I hold the key to the portal I can neither enter nor abandon my post. For this reason when a seeker comes knocking, I demand a boon: A story for safe passage.

Come along then. Join me in my travels beyond the gloom.

Chapter 1

Conversion

I met this bloke in the first decade of my exile from home. It had not occurred to me to demand tales at this time. I busily cataloged the items already stored on the many shelves inside the supposedly famed Arcadium Autum Emporium (it means a hall for selling and trading). Everlander arrived tired and disheveled. He had no interest in buying anything. He merely wanted safe passage through the portal.

I said, "But sir, what does it profit if I allow you through without payment? Have you nothing to give?"

And this is how he changed my life, changed my perspective and gave me a purpose.

Everlander said, "Aye, I have walked among the Dreamers Void. One such dream took me to a strange and alternate future unlike any other I had ever sampled. If you will let me tell you this tale, perhaps if it intrigues you, then you will let me be on my way?"

Now, as I said, trading stories for passage had never entered my mind, but the thought of learning something new and exciting, something that could relieve me from my mundane existence filled me with such a hunger I could not dust off a seat swiftly enough.

Her flesh jiggled with delicate beauty as tears fell to her cheek. As the starlet stood there looking out at the audience, André felt as if she were looking directly at him. Her massive chest heaved, and her dress swirled gracefully. Her lover lay dead upon the floor. The song ended with a grand sigh. The aria had been drawn out adroitly by Miranda Hoffmeister the newest sensation on film. André left the playhouse with visions of plump flesh spilling over the top of the Victorian gown cinched tightly about the remarkable girth of the beauteous star.

Rotund was a state sought after. Ever since the technological advances fostered in the 1850's took hold, the wealthy asserted it was their right to deny the less fortunate souls of the world access. Access to the fortune and knowledge, which would allow all to glow with greasy pinkness, remained tightly controlled.

Hungary boasted themselves as the birthplace of the meat plants, quickly dubbed Fleischgartenen by the German Chancellor, who imported the technology to Cologne. The elite clamored to have dishes prepared by the finest chefs their money could afford. Soon, Flesh Gardens became available worldwide; the multiple meanings only enhanced the appeal.

Over time, the caloric intake doubled, and tripled, as advances in technology allowed the bio-engineered meat to be made even more economically. Nevertheless, it never reached the tables of the masses; Fleischgartens remained a treat for the few and fortunate elite. To double and triple in weight became the accepted model of beauty, one which the poor could never emulate as perfectly as the rich.

On the cusp of the new millennium, André pondered his situation. At the age of twenty years old, he found himself in the reviled state of soon-to-be-homeless. His grades failed to warrant the state paid degree he'd always assumed would be his. His parents were middle class. Middle class meant they were neither skeletal nor rounded. The dream for all remained: to be sufficiently rich enough to gain access to the Flesh Gardens daily.

***

"It's time son," Papa said as he entered André's room.

A lump formed in André's throat as he looked about his room. His bed, piled high with quilts lovingly made by his hard working mother. The walls held pin-ups of his favorite actors and actresses – all pleasingly plump. Nearby, on the nightstand sat his chronometer, he placed it on his wrist, determined to keep what few possessions he could carry with him. Legally, he could visit, but it would be an embarrassment to himself and his family. Particularly once he began to waste away, becoming a Grünlich, a Greeny.

His mother dabbed at her eyes; his sister hid her face in her hair. Maria maintained a nicely rounded figure. Mama and Papa always gave her seconds in the hopes she would marry up. Indeed, the number of rolls signified the number of levels one could dream to ascend. Maria displayed three rolls of flesh hanging from her lovely back; her prominent stomach sat proudly beneath her ample bosom. André felt a stab of jealousy, yet he knew that this was the way of the world. Success in life would be up to him.

"Mama, I will write, I promise," he soothed. Taking in the memory of his family, as he looked intently at each face, he knew it would be years before he returned.

She hugged and kissed him, a frown forming as she felt his sharp and bony body beneath her hands. With tears, she recalled the chubby child he had been; such hopes she had pinned on him!

***

André made his way towards the factory district thinking that a job might be available. Seeing the line, he knew that was merely another dream. As he walked to the welfare office, he derisively thought about the national claims of perfection and productivity.

Forms filed and registrations in order allowed him to gain a microchip implant – placed beneath the skin on his hand. The soft part where thumb and forefinger met throbbed a bit after the bulbous nosed nurse shot it into place.

"Now, it's important for you to remember to return every month to renew your vouchers. Embedded within the chip are codes that when scanned will allow you sixty meals and four showers at our public houses." Her plump face mocked him.

Catching a whiff of her cheap perfume he knew she rarely ate at the Flesh Gardens, he wondered where she managed to gain her extra meals.

Now what, André?

A chubby-faced male tapped him as he sat on a bench outside the offices he'd just left. "Hey, you want to make quick cash?"

The youth perked up. "Sure."

"Sell me your implants each month and you'll soon be rolling in it."

"What? For how much?" André was alert but curious.

"Here, follow me."

They barely walked around the corner when the boy said, "Here we are."

The building was clean, as all buildings were throughout the whole of Europe. The introduction of microbiologics, which fed off rubbish, left behind a green dust. The dust easily blew away in the wind, what remained got vacuumed up weekly by street cleaners.

Inside, it was dark and stuffy. André's first thought was to leave, but a firm voice called, "In here."

The chubby male, who had not offered his name, motioned at a half-closed door towards the end of the long hall.

The library held few books as most of the shelves had been cleared away. In their place hung wires and tubes with the newly developed grow lights positioned above in long lines of bright flickering life. Various plants snaked out of vials, dishes, and baskets. The greenery enchanted and somehow soothed André's discomfort.

The owner of the firm voice belonged to a tall, broad body which André instinctively felt attracted to, despite the lack of fleshy softness.

The gentleman's hand extended as he said, "Doctor Gaspar Ebert, please have a seat." He waved towards the table and chairs after releasing the young man's hand.

André sat.

After small pleasantries and learning of André's newly acquired homeless status, Dr. Ebert said, "I understand you would be wary, having just received your meal chip. But, I can offer you far greater opportunities than the state."

André began to ask a question, but the doctor raised his hand for silence. "Let me continue and then you may ask questions. After. As you know, the Fleischgartenen have been in production for decades. I maintain they are obsolete, and we are in need of a revolution. I have significant backing to fund my research. Sell me your chip and agree to act as my steward, shall we say, and I will provide room and board here. We have rooms upstairs, you must share as I have many volunteers, but at least you will not be in the public houses – turning green."

It was true, those who lived off the state's bounty tended to have a green cast to them, due to the lack of showers and the biologics which fed off the filth of the unwashed. The other option was the military and André did not feel inclined to take that step yet. It was usually the last resort. Prussia flexed its mighty arm, and talks of expansion resounded weekly in shops and news clips. War lingered on the minds of many.

Dr. Ebert continued, "The revolution has already begun, really. In America, they have rejected our accepted form of beauty, "largess" as they call it is passé. And yes, they have taken the word and transformed its meaning…"

Interrupting, André spouted, "What about Hollywood? I have not seen any thin stars on the screen; unless you count the comedians."

"Yes, well the elite of American society tend to emulate those in Europe. But the main core of the continent has found healthy living desirable. This healthful lifestyle is my goal; to expand the Prussian rule and dominance through the Fabian dream." He sighed when he saw the youth had never heard of the acclaimed Fabian Society.

"The Fabian Society espouses simple living, none of this excess and debauchery. It's a quiet revolution, not meant to send citizens to the streets in anger, but to meet the movers and manipulators head on, countering their agendas. The Society gained their ideals from our own beloved Bismark. But not enough has been done. I believe that merely seeing truly healthy males like myself will evolve ones thinking. In time, the ideal model of health will be you and me. For now, we would like to send you into the Fleischgartenen as a waiter."

It was mind blowing to André; he had grown up thinking he was ugly and scrawny. Laughed at by his chubby peers, he had become withdrawn, reticent to act out, or even stand up for himself. Yet a raging hatred simmered within. This idea of change appealed to him.

"I'm interested, but what do you need my meals for?"

"We don't need your meals. We need the chips. I know how to make them, but do not have access to the materials at present. So I buy them, replace the shell, and when you return the attendants remove them and throw them in the trash. You get a new one, and I pay you again for the inner device."

"So wouldn't it make more sense for me to eat most of the meals before I sell the chip?"

Dr. Ebert boomed loudly in response, a chuckle so humorous André could not help but smile in return.

"That's what I liked about you André; always thinking."

"Wait–liked?"

The doctor nodded his head, "Yes, we engineered your failing grade. Wait, please sit! It was done so you could gain a superior education here–with me." He waved towards the hydroponics.

"You had no right!" André screamed, he felt spittle spray as he yelled his frustration at this stranger.

The doctor sat serenely as though this had happened before. André was quick to note the doctors' calm demeanor and asked, "So how many did you say you have abducted?"

"Please, do soothe yourself. I am offering you a chance to be part of the avant-garde few who will change society for the better. Stay with us this night. Should you choose to reject this kind offer I can look into reversing your grades–it will be seen as a slight misunderstanding–a lost paper."

Andre had toured the public-house earlier and was loathe to spend the night there when he had an alternative. Before him sat an opportunity to be tutored directly by an evidently well-read and powerful scientist. He could at least spend the night and give his answer in the morning.

Chubby-face came in and introduced himself as Blaine. Taking him upstairs, he said, "This will be your room, you will share it with me."

Great, thought André. *Now I get to be humiliated by staying with a pleasantly plump boy while he makes fun of my slight frame.* He was, of course, nowhere near the famed girth of the rich and famous. Twenty stone was the magic number many worked so hard to attain. Rumors swirled that the very elite sported thirty or more, but that was laughed off as wives' tales or folly.

"Okay, now what?" André asked.

"Now we get dressed for work."

The expression on André's face required an answer, so Blaine continued, "We will wait on the tables among the rich and famous within Cologne's very finest Fleischgarten, you may have heard of it, *La Récompense de Gluttons.*"

Dressed in plain white shirts with stiff collars, and black woolen pants, the pair joined others on a trolley headed uptown.

André had, of course, seen edited scenes of the rich eating within the famed La Récompense de Gluttons but never did he expect to view such opulence in person.

The Greek architecture of the building featured female figures for columns. André had always found it ironic that the house of gluttons had such slim women holding the building up. The building was old, having been built before the advent of meat plants.

The smell was divine; André hoped he would be allowed to eat before being made to serve all night.

Blaine laughed and brought him to the day old food bin. The meat was cold, but looked delicious, once their plates were loaded with scoops of this and that, Blaine showed André how easily the warming ovens worked–another new technology, not yet available to the masses–waves of energy shot through the box, heating the food internally.

Hungrily, they each scarfed down the food, finishing just as their supervisor arrived to train the three new workers.

Once given instructions on behaviors and swiftness, it was time to work. Andre entered and found the immense space quite daunting; it reminded him of Greek and Roman temples. Indeed, he thought he should bow before the goddess of flesh that he was asked to serve. She appeared, and he later learned it was true, to have grown in place upon her throne.

She was barely clothed, dressed in a toga to match the decor, the folds of her skin seemed to go on forever. Never had André thought such a feat possible. Her golden hair shone with angelic luster; her ruby lips glistened from the grease of her previous meal.

How could my small frame ever be something to be desired? André wondered. *This woman is glorious!*

She ordered everything on the menu, it took him all night to serve her and her alone. The more she ate, the more André lost his reverence. He still saw her as lovely for that had been ingrained from birth. *Surely such excess is wrong?* She ate enough to feed his family for two days! Handmaids came in between rounds and washed her clean. The delicately crafted dishes hardly seemed to merit appreciation as she tore them apart to devour with slurping gasps of engorgement.

The former supplicant lowered his eyes out of repulsive horror rather than deference. Unsure of whether he wanted to eat the grease slathered flesh again, André worked to maintain a calm exterior.

Gaspar Ebert observed from a darkened corner; the flared nostrils and bobbing Adam's apple on the youth brought a smile. Another convert had been born.

Chapter 2

Walking in the Way

Half the time I never understood why anyone would even want to use the portal that I guarded. I couldn't even explain to myself why I would want to. It leads to home, the only home I ever knew. The Goblin King is my father, not by blood, mind. He "adopts" countless children. I never fit in. Literally, I was too tall, gangly is how my nanny termed it. Ha, most likely my lanky self inspired the previous tale. Now this one is mighty peculiar. I was unaware of Humans having the ability to use portals at all. But this man, a mere Human, entered and instead of searching among my vast emporium, he straight away requested access to the portal.

Said I, "Blimey, mate. Do ye know where this here portal leads?"

He raised his hoary head and with still sharp, clear blue eyes aimed at mine he replied, "I've been told it leads to The Goblin King."

Before demanding his story I replied, "Aye, it could at that."

It's not well known, this teleporting, but once learned seeking new portals becomes an obsession. For me at any rate. I warned my students, back when I had students, about this risk. Very few manage to keep it as a mere pastime.

The ability began in my earliest years, the obsession too. One minute I was skipping down the sidewalk making sure I missed each and every crack when suddenly I found myself standing by the giant oak tree in the back school yard. Now a normal child would have screamed and ran home yelling for mommy. But I didn't know I was supposed to be frightened of such things and merely whispered a near silent, "Whoa!" and then added, "How do I get back?"

Being only six, I couldn't figure it out. Still, I did learn the pattern of my skipping soon enough and could get myself to school in no time flat. Mom often hollered at me to hurry or I'd be late for school. In reality, I was almost always one of the first to arrive.

By the age of eight, I finally figured out the pathway back to my house, it was more tricky than avoiding cracks in a certain pattern, yet still used a similar principle. The ground was riddled with gnarled roots snaking out and away from the tree. Trial, after trial, I learned that I needed to approach the tree from the south, where the woods grew thicker beyond the school property. Then, I needed to step on the roots in a particular pattern rather than avoid them which had been my first thought. It became another game of sorts, leaping from root to root as I researched alone beneath the tree for those two years. I carefully scribbled what did not work in a little pocket-sized notebook. Trust me, I tried hundreds of version from each angle.

Success was not denied me. Thankfully, none were watching me behind the tree. If anyone had chanced to glanced over, they would have thought I was simply up in the tree, or hidden by the trunk. Arriving on the sidewalk surprised me as I popped up just behind the mailman as he left my house, making his way to the Finklemeyer's.

He was fairly new on the route, having been at it for six months. I tried to be there at the mailbox to say "hi" to him all summer. He was kind and often handed me a post card addressed to me. Once I grew older, I realized not every kid gets post cards from their mailman. Mr. Radcliffe is a cherished memory in my heart.

I maintained a habit of watching the people on the sidewalk just to see if any of them ever winked out of existence. They never did. . . in fact, it further annoyed my little sensibilities when it appeared some of them made it a point to deliberately step on the cracks! I almost took it personally but did not want to reveal such emotions or even get close to telling about my discovery. So I stifled the outrage and allowed discontent to flow over me.

Spinning about, the mailman's eyes were wide with apparent fright. I assumed he thought a rabid dog was about to bite him, but then his eyes narrowed and scanned the area for observers.

"Timmy, I would advise against such shenanigans in broad daylight."

That's all he said and then resumed his letter sorting as he made his way to the next mail box.

I thought about what he said but did in no way want to be tardy to afternoon classes so ensuring his back remained turned, I skipped the pattern towards the portal, returning just as the bell signaling the end of recess sounded sweet raucousness to my ears.

I smiled the rest of the day. My secret was not mine alone;

somehow others could do it too! The mailman would become my new best friend. I determined I would convince him to spill what he knew.

Indeed a secret order of Travelers do exist, but it took five years before Mr. Radcliffe agreed to take me to a meeting. I was thirteen, and he used the excuse of hiring me for yard work. Mother was delighted and waved me off with smiles and a bag of peanut butter cookies.

It felt mildly uncomfortable being the youngest one there, but I did like adults a bit more than children. They soon ceased their superior poses as they listened to my tale of how I discovered the portals.

Better than anything, they freely shared the patterns for the portals they had discovered! Who would have thought such kindness existed in this world of ours? Of course, I was sworn to secrecy and became the youngest member ever initiated into the *Society of the Way.*

Since I am sharing this tale, you may as well know I did, over the years, discover new paths on my own, some I kept just to myself. I assume the same has been done by the others. At the time I believed all was goodness and light. Suffice it to say, darkness found me, eventually.

One of the last secrets revealed to me as I left my teenage years was the truth that some patterns are always exactly the same. Such as when walking a pattern on a checkered floor. It's more like a dance step and involves a bit of leaping so, for good reason, those patterns are mainly done only by night guards at the mall or in private homes. Fortunately, no portal ever leads to an inherently dangerous place.

Then again, the night guard taking the leap may very well find himself locked out of his place of employment, thus walking one of the many patterns upon tile is rarely done. I shared this tale with my grandson; as you can see I am quite old. I felt a need to leave my patterns to someone and who better than my own dear grandson? He who on his own, like me, discovered the joys of Walking in the Way.

***

I must say the story astounded me. As I said, I never knew Humans could use these "magical" portals. Indeed most of the forms of portals he mentioned are not even known by the Faire. Fairies and Elves and the like use portals of their own making to get to places they have been to before. They also have five or so fixed portals much like the one I oversee. Though most of theirs go to the Land of Eternal Spring . . . tra la la and all that rot.

I asked him more pointedly, "What business do ye have with the King?"

A wan smile settled on his wrinkled face. "None, really. I have reached the end of my years and did not wish to die at home. Seeking portals remains my obsession. I have gone through every portal I have ever learned of. I saved this one for last."

Now a blokes got to admire a man seeking the King's favor. As a gift of my own, I handed the Walker of the Way a gift for him to pass along to my father. If he managed to make it that far, it may have spared him a little longer.

With jealousy and trepidation I opened the portal and waved him through. I never wish a guy luck. There's no such thing in the underworld.

Chapter 3

Qu'est-ce que c'est

Speaking of the underworld. This story is quite recent but the last story reminded me of it so I will share it now. He claimed to be a worshipper of The Ruler of the Underworld. Personally, I thought he was insane before he even told me his story . . . truth be told, his tale did nothing to change my assessment.

He believed he was Death incarnate. He arrived in a black hooded robe, indeed he wore a glamor that flickered between his real self, a mongrel Troll mixed-with-what I could not tell, and the mask he wore which was indeed a skeletal visage. One might assume Death would wear such a face to collect souls. In the gloom he looked like a talking head.

Of a truth, I have collected a few tales from others who also purported to be Death incarnate. I'll let you judge which might be true.

Gladly, I rid this psycho killer from my presence. Honestly, I could not trust his actions as he seemed as if he might lose control at any moment. Thankfully, his tale was short.

Showered, shaved and dressed for bed, I turned out the bathroom light as a thought entered my head, unbidden:

Run . . .

Moreover . . . *Run!*

Resisting the urge, I crawled into bed, a smile stretching wide as I met my wife there. A smile meant to please and comfort, yet it failed to reach my eyes. I could feel it.

Shifting away from her pink lace and flower scented person, I noted the shadows dancing on the wall. She had lit candles, vanilla and jasmine.

I wanted to scream: *Run!* But I wasn't sure who should be doing the running. Inhaling deeply I tried to relax, tension was building, and I could not seem to shake off the impending doom I felt.

Repeating her question from earlier she asked, "Well, do you like it?"

Her green eyes were wide and intense, lined in turquoise and painted gold. Her lips were baby soft, pink, and slick with moisture, meant to invite passion.

Lips had remained pressed when she had asked that first time. Why did she bother asking again? I had heard the first time . . . and yet she failed to recognize her error.

My eyes burned into her, I could feel myself burning up lying there in bed, skin-to-skin with my lover. *Why is she still talking?* I saw her lips moving but couldn't hear a thing . . . nothing except: *Run, run, run . . .*

My rough hands caressed her face, her question still in her glance, but her smile had left. To appease, I looked at the new tattoo . . . it was me. How could she have known?

For I am hidden deep within his head and soul.

There . . . that scream once more . . . *Run!* He struggles to escape, to warn her.

No, he didn't have the chance, he was blind, vainly thinking he could control me. Ha! *Me* the monster within, a death-mask now marking her breast, my semblance, her desire.

Dance with me O death, she sang

Delight me with your skill

Dandle me upon your knee

My love you'll never kill

I could grasp it now . . . this thought screaming from within. It would have been far, far better for her had she run when he'd told her. The shadows dance, the jasmine swirls, twining with vanilla and lust. Fingers tangle through her golden red hair her response fuels my desire.

On fire . . . the bed's a pyre, built like an altar to me. No sleeping tonight as I fight, and I fight, against myself and the being within. We cannot agree. He wants to be free, to run, oh to run and be done. Our life is not easy, not easy at all. But he'll fall as I call for his silence.

What is it? What is it? What do we desire?

This fire it's building within, this molten inferno must surely erupt! To quench it, to wrench it away from my heart—there is but one thing to be done. Such fun . . . I clasp her fragile frame and embrace the inevitable death. The wife's done away, now we can play . . .

In hopes of glory, we run . . .

Chapter 4

A Moment With Death

I had not had a visitor for a month when he arrived. His death mask was absolutely convincing. I almost felt a sense of relief that my torture was over. But he lowered his hood and his mask vanished, leaving a normal looking Human standing there.

"Didn't mean to frighten you, it's just easier to travel within my aspect's power than it is to drive up, park the car, and come in through the door. I'm in a bit of a hurry."

I smirked as I refused entrance without payment.

Sighing, he took out a pocket watch, clicked it and looked about for a seat. "Before I begin," said he, "I need to know if it is indeed possible to find Ambrosia, the nectar of the gods, within the Underworld. I have heard Persephone offers it to select guests."

I felt my brow furrow. It seemed to me that in the second century of my watchman's duties, more people knew what I assumed to be private matters concerning Goblins and the Underworld. I blurted, "Who told you that?"

Death smiled back, his mask wavered briefly presenting a deathly white skull. "Satan was chatting a bit after hours and he mentioned he'd been served the drink at a summer party he'd attended years ago. Do you want to hear how I became Death or not?"

Pushing aside my concern, I nodded and waved him on.

Sweet ambrosia! That was my first thought when I saw her that very first time. Not that I knew what ambrosia was. She sat softly weeping over her soon to be departed father. The sun shone in from the setting sun, giving a golden glow to her already golden brown curls. Even there in the hospital, her scent was noticeable, citrus touched with coconut. So angelic!

Her father did not die that night as doctors came in and hooked him up to life support. That really puts me off schedule when doctors do that, but this time I did not mind. It meant I could return to look at her again. On my third visit, her father was

released as they removed the life support. Ensnaring his evenly gray spirit in my gloved fingers, I folded it compactly to place within my satchel. All the while gazing upon her downcast head. Her slim shoulders shook with grief. Then she looked up taking note of my presence.

"Is death painful?"

"Do you see me?" I asked.

"Well, of course, I see you. I do not make it a habit to speak to thin air."

Her caustic nature caught me off guard, as it did not fit with my imagined angelic thoughts of her. Too I sorrowed, for only those close to death can see me.

"Death itself is not painful, but the moments before can be quite torturous depending on your method of departure."

She laughed! I did not know how to take her, but her laugh was so delightful I could not help but want to hear it again.

She was contemplating suicide, as nothing at all was wrong with her health. I convinced her to delay her actions if she would allow me to visit her. Often. Laughing in delight, she exclaimed, "Sure it's perfect, I have a date with Death!"

We started dating, it has now been nine months since we began our relationship. She is still suicidal, which causes me to hasten to her side at inopportune times, and yet I cannot fault her, for it keeps us close. I searched the archives to find out if the ambrosia of the gods is real, giving it to her would be my greatest pleasure. To live for centuries with her by my side without the fear of losing her, ah to dream!

Last night I met with her again. My patience with my work was thinning, yet I had one final assignment for the day.

Mounting my pale horse, I made my way to the home of a woman in need of meeting her destiny. Not all cases need personal attention, fortunately. Were that the case I'd beg the powers that be for assistants. So I'm it, Death. The Grim Reaper, also known as Azriel. I've only been doing this for a year. The previous guy retired and chose me, Draper, seemingly at random.

As my horse climbed the steep mountain path, my mind wandered back to my own meeting of destiny. Life had been at a standstill. Getting fired had been the last of my troubles. A broken engagement and the death of my parents meant I saw no more reasons to stay. With no one to turn to, feeling lost and dejected I made a decision. At my height of despair, Azriel walked in to collect my soul, taking a pocket watch out from an inner pocket of his black robe, he clicked it and nodded with a satisfied bob of his head.

I had just slit my wrist and knew surely I was not yet dead. The blood welled up and then froze, like a still life. Neither pain nor relief flooded my senses. Curiosity and even puzzlement filled me, as the specter pushed his hood back and the death mask dissipated. Before me stood a young man— younger than myself.

"This is death?" I asked.

The near specter shrugged, and replied, "Not quite. I am Azriel, the Grim Reaper personified. I have put time on hold."

"Why? I have no wish to remain here!"

"I understand. Once, I was in your place. I've been monitoring you and feel I have found the right man."

"The right man for what?" I felt a tingle run up my spine as I envisioned tortures and more.

As it was, Azriel tired of being Death and wished to retire. He proposed trading places, explaining it was possible since he had swapped out with his predecessor when he was trying to commit suicide long centuries past. Obviously, I accepted.

Reaching my destination I stopped my reminiscing. The home sat precariously on the side of the mountain, a young mother was alone with her child, depression filled her soul. With no means of support, her husband had been drafted, she'd had no response from him for months. He would not be returning. She was mother of a newborn, too weak to go down the mountain to see a village doctor, and too poor to pay for the services anyway. Out of food, and with the ground still frozen there was no hope of finding any.

A year earlier I had a hard time taking lives so sadly and permanently wasted. Having since gained an understanding, I calmly entered, only to see she had a laser weapon, her child already vaporized. Being an infant it in no way needed to be taken by Death. I watched as the mother sobbed and prayed, seeking forgiveness while unseen by her eyes, the infant's spirit ascended to heaven. Then turning the gun inward, her sad face disappeared, leaving her body and spirit. The wispy gossamer essence was easily snared by Death's clawed grasp. Because she was neither pure nor easily condemnable, her spirit hung in the balance, these are they whom Death must collect.

By the way, call me Thanatos.

Folding her spirit like a package, I placed it in my pouch, and with a sigh of relief, my shift was over.

Thankful that I am not charged with judgment I deposited the collected souls and returned home to my well-appointed apartment. Yes, being the Grim Reaper is grim. But it has its perks.

Feeling duplicitous, I offered a small vial of Fairy Dust to Death. "This is quite valuable and a little goes a long way. A few shakes of the stuff on your clothes and any requests you make will be met with less resistance than usual. I suggest you take the first left followed by two rights."

I do love happy endings and hope filled me that he would manage to get the Ambrosia.

Chapter 5

Death Cheats No One

Weeks later, Death stood outside the portal, requesting swift passage back into the everyday world. On principle, I always demand a second tale from those seeking reentry. The blighter was cheeky and told a very short tale. No matter how much I begged, he refused to tell me of his adventures in the underworld.

Success was his, his sweetheart would join him permanently without death. I shudder to think what deals he made. But he is Death after all and has his own powerful bargaining chips to play.

It stabs fresh wounds upon my soul when visitors return without news from my father. His silence pains my weak heart. I enjoyed living among the Goblins. But once I hit my teenage years my body kept growing and growing. Father even built new living quarters. . . upsized to match my recalcitrant height.

Usually when the Goblin King "adopts" children, his magic allows him to transform them to match the normal five inch height of most Goblins. For some reason my body repels that magic. After years of cruel taunts from my siblings in the King's household, I was reassigned to my current post. It is not fair! I know very well that there are several communities where everyone employs full Human stature in the Underworld. Father is NOT the only ruler down below. Thanatos and many other visitors prove this point.

Thanotos stepped into the room.

In the grips of death, her husband lay, unconscious and unaware of her pleas. She was fair to look upon, sweetly plain, yet attractive, her hair unbound and free.

The specter was loathe to grant her petition, experience informed his reticence.

Nevertheless, it was soon thrown at his feet. Lifting flashing green eyes, rimmed hot and pink, she startled, cruel recognition severe on her face. The pale figure dressed in black stood silently awaiting his duty.

Clutching her husband she yelled, "No, do not take him! He has dreams to fulfill."

Death stepped closer, his quota to keep.

"Please, if you must harvest a soul this night, be quick, but let it be mine. I cannot bear to live with out my love. Speak, foul fiend! Do you hear me?"

Feigned bravery, soon wavered to flutters. Her beauty enraptured Death. Her dressing gown fell open as she knelt before him. Her sheer gown beneath reminded him of angel's robes. Yes, her act of love would win her a place on high.

Thanatos replied, "I hear you woman. Is this your heart's desire?" He held aloft, the symbol of his office, his scythe. It hung in the air darkly above her head.

With quivering resolve she nodded once, bowing herself to the ground. Her lips moving in supplication. Swiftly, Thanatos snared her soul with skeletal fingers. The gauzy fabric of her being wavered mere moments in silence, before ascending up through the ceiling.

Thanatos sighed as duty beckoned, with one backward glance at life reprieved he departed.

Experience spoke, Death would be back at dawn.

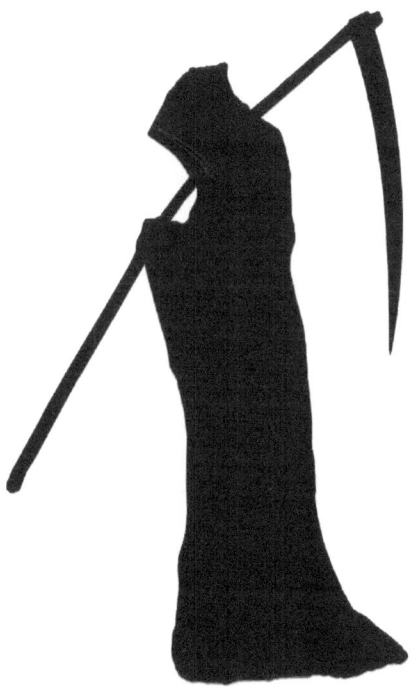

Chapter 6

Hippety-Hop, Hippety-Hop

I must confess I rather liked this tale. A sweet blonde woman came into the shop, an Elf really. She told this tale with a smirk the whole way through. Once done, I begged to know whether she had made it up.

She replied, "In a manner of speaking. By entering his dream implanted the "memory" within. He had it coming. I infer his thoughts based on my observations."

Obviously, I wanted to know more but was denied, one story was the price and she refused to say more.

One line in particular enchanted me: The day was bright and the air was mild. It triggered a far off memory of my own, from before. Before I was snatched from my crib to live forever in the shadows. Never again have I walked beneath the blue skies of earth. I do have a small window upstairs that is not tinted in a myriad of colors like the main shop windows; sitting up there I can gaze out upon the street and see the park across the way. Children play and dogs frolic. And the sky . . . ever changing and deeply inviting.

If only . . .

Twaddle

Hippety-Hop, Hippety-Hop

May skipped 'round in a happy, bouncy way

Hippety-Hop, Hippety-Hop

The day was bright and the air was mild

Hippety-Hop, Hippety-Hop

Oh, May was such an endearing child

Hippety-Hop, Hippety-Hop

Her curls flew 'round like a kite tail in play

Hippety-Hop, Hippety-Hop

Twaddle

This is what went through his mind like a repeating video; over and over it played. He tried to make it stop by getting involved in other activities. It worked. But as soon as he stopped. There. Yes, just like that it returned, twaddle. Twaddle! What kind of word is that anyhow?

He sat. He knew he shouldn't, sitting made it go faster. Hippety-Hop, Hippety-Hop!

Ahhh, he wanted to scream, yet he kept it all in. What would people think of him if they knew? With a sigh he got up.

"Where are you off to now? Can't you sit still more than ten seconds!" she said.

He looked at her, his wife, her lovely form snuggled all cozy on the couch. It was spring and the nights were still cool. Her least of all would he tell.

"I just forgot something in the car. I'll be right back, sweetie." He kissed her as he made for the door. "I won't be long, I promise."

Twaddle

Hippety-Hop . . .

He sat in the car and turned on the radio. Loud. He screamed. He sang. He banged to the tune until he realized he was going Hippety-Hop Hippety-Hop.

He squeezed his eyes shut and held back the sob. "I can deal with this," he said.

He got out just as his sweetheart was opening the side door.

"I'm coming. No worries, go ahead and put the movie in. I'll make popcorn."

He busied himself in the kitchen until she called, anxiously telling him he was going miss the beginning. He had prepared a tray of goodies. Popcorn, of course but he had also found M&M's and Skittles. He made a little snack mix by adding pretzels and Chex cereal plus the last of the peanuts.

"I'm coming, I'm coming. Twaddle! I didn't miss a thing!"

She smirked at him and took a handful of popcorn.

Saturdays were almost the worst. No structure allowed for a lot of empty minded nothing. Only his mind was filled with a vision of a sweet little girl named May. She was barely five years old and lived next door. Her golden curls tended to tangle in a way that made him wonder if it had ever been smooth. He longed to reach out and feel the texture. He was sure it was silky soft, maybe like his kitten. She had just learned to skip, and would make her way up and down the block, as carefree as any child could be. No other vision filled his mind so completely as this one did.

Yes, Saturdays were definitely the worst.

Sundays were bad, but not quite so bad since he filled the day with such religious devotion that one would think he dreamed of becoming the next spiritual leader of all mankind. Morning church, afternoon study and evening church filled up a large portion of his day. He fit in visits to the animal shelter, as well as the retirement center; where he played the piano for the enjoyment of the residents. Playing the piano helped. Yes, getting lessons was surely a good use of his time as a youth.

Piano lessons helped him forget.

Forget what?

Hippety-Hop, Hippety-Hop . . .

Oh, yeah that.

Finally, Monday rolled 'round again. His wife was ever amazed that he could find such joy and enthusiasm for going to work. Yet, she said it was one of the things that had attracted her to him. Having dated guys who kept losing their jobs, or nearly as bad; guys with dead end jobs, she was quite taken with the young go-getter. No, he was nothing like those guys. He worked in a plastics manufacturing plant. He was middle management, with the goal of making it to the next tier before thirty.

He hummed as he walked from the car to his office. Ever the same tune; kind of bouncy, something that nearly made one want to hop and skip. He never noticed.

"Hippety-Hop, sir."

"What?" he asked the young assistant who greeted him daily.

"I said,'What's up sir?'" the young adult replied.

"Oh…" He shook his head as if to clear it. "Well, Tim, not much. Today we need to work on that application for the Morrow account and then see what we can devise for that toy company."

He immersed himself in his work and then sorrowfully took himself to his car for the twenty minute drive home. Twaddle! And so it began.

He stopped to buy the groceries his sweet, adoring wife had called to remind him to get. He imagined the sparkle in her eye as he brought her flowers. Nodding, he went to the florist counter.

He thought the sign said, "Hippety-Hop." It didn't disappear when he blinked, so he stopped looking at it. The lady at the counter had large teeth, he stared at them as she said, "The day was bright and the air was mild."

"Yes," he replied, puzzled, "yes, it surely was."

"May I get a dozen daisies, please?" He felt sweat trickling down his back as his eyes chanced upon the words, "Hippety-Hop" not once, but twice.

She replied sadly, "Oh, May was such an endearing child."

Hippety-Hop, Hippety-Hop. Why was it said so sadly? He felt anxious and wiped his face as she passed the wrapped flowers to him with a worried look.

"Her curls flew 'round like a kite tail in play."

He spun around to hear the man behind him intone the final

verse; that last vision which he held so privately. How could they know? How could anyone know?

> Hippety-Hop, Hippety-Hop,
> Twaddle.

He found himself in a room without windows. Rocking to the beat inside his head. A smile tickling his lips...

> Twaddle
>
> Hippety-Hop, Hippety-Hop
>
> May skipped 'round in a happy, bouncy way
>
> Hippety-Hop, Hippety-Hop
>
> The day was bright and the air was mild
>
> Hippety-Hop, Hippety-Hop
>
> Oh, May was such an endearing child
>
> Hippety-Hop, Hippety-Hop
>
> Her curls flew 'round like a kite tail in play
>
> Hippety-Hop, Hippety-Hop
>
> Twaddle

Chapter 7

Not Even a Memory

Speaking of memories. Like those fleeting snatches of sky and rolling in the grass with parents whose faces I cannot conjure. Memories that cause equal amounts of pain and joy. I sat one day discussing life with a frequent visitor, one Miss Terra, in fact.

Terra is a Goblin, she barely stands as tall as my chest. That is rather tall for a Goblin though, so she quite enjoys commiserating with me about our height.

Over tea, Terra shared this tale about a Human that she studied during her schooling. A few rare Goblins manage to attend the Fair Realms Academy in England. Terra proved herself of worth before the Goblin King as well as the board of education admissions committee. Stuffing away my jealousy is the only way I have been able to continue our friendship. Where was I? Oh, yes. Terra was able to study this Human and willingly told me this story without demands of passage.

Despite the simpleness of this story, the horror of his ordeal troubled me for days.

Simeon knew he should have looked, but he was in a hurry. Forever after, he thought about what could have been, had he taken those few moments to turn his eyes.

Life for Simeon had been pleasant; he had been an average student, had gotten a degree in accounting, and had found a job in the insurance office not far from his apartment. Occasionally, he went out on Friday or Saturday night. He saw her around town with other friends he had gone to school with. Simeon recalled thinking about asking her out.

More than thinking really, it impinged on his ability to complete his work in a timely manner. Not that he lost his job or anything . . . He just got passed over for promotions.

Getting the courage took a year as he spent every day dreaming about her.

With him.

Her long, strawberry blonde hair reflected the sun as he sat in the park with Muriel, the girl of his dreams, looking at her in wonder. Such luck! Simeon was in love and amazed to hear her say she loved him too. Muriel agreed to marry him and soon they were happily planning their wedding.

Nothing made Simeon happier than to give the petite imp of a woman the fairytale wedding she deserved. He dreamed of the day they would be united as one . . . both were virgins.

He reveled in the softness of her pale ivory skin. Her face had the lightest smattering of freckles which she allowed him to count as he tried to kiss each one individually.

Simeon never understood what she saw in him, what with his lanky frame and large Adam"s apple. He felt awkward and clumsy as a young adult. Muriel said he was sleek and wiry and reminded her of her favorite literary character, some elf he could not recall.

Now he sat – contemplating the calamity that his inattention had caused. What beauty and joy had been his! With bittersweet emotions, he recalled their wedding day. He had been so in awe of her as she came down the aisle.

"Soon!" he thought, "All I have ever dreamed of will be mine."

The party had gone smoothly, family behaved, the dancing was perfect, his desire was becoming nearly impossible to contain. He convinced her to leave an hour sooner than planned. With joy and tears, their parents and friends waved them off to their new life, as husband and wife.

Oh, the injustice of it all! The bitterness that filled Simeon now was as strong as the joy and anticipation he had felt then as they entered their hotel suite. He did not wait for her to change, pulling her to the bed they fell into each others arms. He reveled in her green-gray eyes held wide, as she drank him in.

The tragedy.

Simeon had not looked, he never saw the oncoming car which took away his ability to walk, but worse, far worse it stole his memories.

Those beautiful eyes looked at him now, with love and concern in a pleasantly aged face. She told him they had been married twenty-three years, and yet he could only recall those first few kisses on their wedding night. His passion and desire for her consumed him, and he had nothing – not even a memory.

Not even a memory…

Chapter 8

I Was A Teenage Runaway

Portals are an interesting phenomena. In all the studying I have done, and I have managed quite a bit despite not attending any of the fine Academies for those like me, in all of my studies I have never learned who found the portals first.

The Fairies have Fairy doors. Water Sprites have a few portals that take them into the Land of Eternal Spring, and I have heard tell that Mermaids even have access to Atlantis, not lost to them at all. Among my studies I have learned that Time Travel is indeed possible through select portals from within the Void.

The Void is another tale altogether, but essentially Fair Ones have access to the Void through their Dreams. Using properties that I have yet to discover, some Elves have managed to learn how to use the Land of Eternal Spring in order to shift their own person through various times.

I think if I learned this wee bit of knowledge, Father would release me from this task. At any rate a Visitor (from another planet) shared this tale with me back in 1958.

I found myself leaving after three years of living there. My dad liked to move often, it was actually the longest we had stayed at any one place. The fear that we would be leaving soon made it hard for me to accept that we might be staying, so I never allowed any real friendships to develop with the kids at school.

Life at home really wasn't horrible; I just didn't like it anymore. Dad was hardly ever home since he went off to make money wherever that was. I didn't know, I never paid attention to what he did. He wore nice clothes and slicked his red hair back. I don't think he spoke to me but once a week. I told myself that he wouldn't miss me.

Mom had left us when we lived in Orlando. I was six. I figured she thought, since I was in school, I didn't need her. My older brother was nine, he's eighteen now, a senior. Yeah, that makes me fifteen. I know it's a bit young to be out on my own, alright a lot young, but seriously! He was a jerk of a big brother, and I was just tired of the loneliness I felt.

Okay, here's the thing. Life on the streets is tough. I started out hiding in the bus depot; it's warm at night, and at least the seats are cushioned. But they go around and chase people off every couple of hours, so, you know, it gets tiring. I hadn't had a good night's sleep for four months. No, I did not stay in the same town when I ran away. I was one hundred miles away, so yeah, I could've gone home easily enough–had I wanted.

I called once, last week since I'd been thinking of them. But the line was disconnected. What a jerk my dad is! He couldn't even stay through the year to let my brother graduate; Brady had been happy there, even if I was not. Graduation would be this week.

No telling where Dad drug them off to.

Yeah, yeah, I know this is dragging on I'm getting to the good part! Just listen.

Okay, so after I called home, I felt worse than ever. Well, wouldn't you? I bet they never even reported me missing. So I was walking downtown and saw Crazy Jim heading my way. When they say crazy they mean it; he will grab a hold of ya and spew his stinking breath all over you while ranting about spies and secret plots against mankind.

The first time he caught me I nearly threw up, he stank so horribly. Bleh! He was going on and on about some scientific research he claimed the government was conducting, involving time travel and mutants. I don't know, he was a madman, and I was frantically trying to find out how to get away from him. Then a young guy appeared, not much older than me, he tapped Crazy Jim on the shoulder, allowing me to escape.

Believe me, I ran! But the guy, the young one, had eyes of gold which pierced my consciousness. I have not been able to get him out of my thoughts. Four weeks have passed since that time. I walked all over town hoping I would run into him. I know you are thinking – who wants to hook up with a girl on the streets? But listen. I never looked bad. I managed to get into the shelter twice a week where I could shower and pick up clean clothes. It's not like I lived out of my backpack exclusively. That is, once I finally found the shelter. I got food there at least once a day and the rest I panhandled; I made maybe twenty dollars a day, it really worked out well. But like I said, I was tired.

Okay, so picture this: I am walking downtown, and Crazy Jim has his eye on me. I panic. It's rush hour and cars are all over the road–so I can't run across to the other side. I was not next to a store so I couldn't go inside either. It's an apartment building. So the only thing was to go into the ally.

I hate alleys. In small towns they are okay, kind of quiet, you know? They make good shortcuts. But in the cities they stink, trash is strewn about, they are dark and have lots of hiding places. Just what I needed, but who knew what else was hiding in there?

Imagine this: My breathing gets loud, I hear myself softly whining. I risk looking back, and sure enough, he's there. He has a bad leg, so he is slow, but still, he is making his way towards me. And yeah, like you thought, it's a dead end ally. The apartments have a fence blocking the way into the courtyard.

A darkened doorway is the only place to hide. Not good enough I know, but it's my only option, so I stumble up the steps and cower there. I try to still my breathing as I hear Crazy Jim babbling, stumping his way towards me.

"They will get you. They always get what they want. Trust me, your dad knew what he was doing. You should've stayed."

My Dad? I think. *No, he's crazy.* I bang on the door hoping some janitor would be on the other side. Crazy Jim starts up the stairs, I could smell his stench already.

I open my mouth to scream when the door opens by sliding sideways. "Mr. Golden eyes" captures my attention as he pulls me in. Safe, I felt safe. The door slid shut as Crazy Jim cackled, "They always get what they want."

The guy felt so good. I held on longer than was necessary. After a bit he shifted, letting me know I needed to stop being silly. I realized that the place was well lit and new looking, contrasting with the ancient exterior. I say new, but it had an old time feel to it.

You know, like what you see in old black and white movies, high class, but old style. Oh, well, you know what I mean; Cary Grant flair.

The boy with the golden eyes guided me to a sitting room.

It finally registered that this was all very odd. I *can* be dense.

"Who are you?" I asked fearfully, while admiring his sleek body.

"My name is Thomas. I am sorry that Jim frightened you like that. We have been trying to contact you for ages."

Signals fired off in my brain, but who knows what it meant. He smiled and offered me a soda.

Thomas continued,"Let me explain a few things, Jim is not entirely crazy. We are involved with time travel experiments. Here . . ." he pointed at his feet and gestured at the walls round about, "we are in 1952, out there, it is 2010."

My face went slack.

"You do not belong in that time, neither you nor your family. Your father is a respected scientist. He took off one day with some important pieces of research, which we need back. If you will help us locate him, we can offer you a comfortable retirement package."

Just then my mother entered the room. I was in shock as she hugged me with tear-filled eyes. My father had lied! My mother had not run off, she had returned to her own time! My head hurt. They lead me to a clean room with a soft bed. I slept for hours. More hours than I knew possible. It was glorious.

When I woke, my mother took me home. I mean my real home, the one I vaguely remembered from when I was four. My room is still papered with large cabbage roses, and soft green curtains hang from the windows.

She enrolled me in school even though only three weeks are left until summer vacation.

So here I am at your little bonfire party, thanks for inviting me by the way. But my question is–Am I crazy or did this really happen?

Chapter 9

Happy Hunting

One thing I appreciate about my confinement here in the Arcadium is the freedom to study every book in the vast collection along the eastern wall. Granted very few books are filled with actual stories. But I am pleased to report that I had learned about how werewolves were created long before I heard this tale.

Briefly, I learned that Visitors from another planet, or rather a set of planets, came here for scientific purposes. They were not content to merely witness the natural state of the flora and fauna, these Visitors often tweaked DNA here and there. So it was during the Greek and Roman's early years that wolf-men were created.

I collected this story quite recently, in 2018, in fact. How much was true and how much was made up was not easy for me to divine. The Fae telling the tale has been known for ages for her flights of fancy, as it were.

Intense.

That is how Bucky would have described the moment. The glow of the sun lingered upon the western horizon, and the low moon taunted her three-quarter face in brilliant copper. The pull of the moon became distracting, yet not enough to relinquish his prize.

There it was, stark white against the dark mountainside. A beautiful bighorn ram. Having tracked it for days, essentially herding it to this location–prime for the kill. Crouching low . . .

Bam!

A shot rang out, and the sheep went hurtling down the side of the mountain to land on the ledge twenty feet below.

Disoriented at first and then enraged, Bucky sought after the man who had taken his prize. A deep growl emanated from his throat as he aimed his attack, mauling the man viciously before gaining control of his actions.

Having stopped, he surveyed the damage. Fully in control once again, he lapped at the bloody mess delicately, then lay down to wait.

***

Grady heard himself moan before his vision cleared. Moving sent fire coursing through his body, so he lay still trying understand why he hurt so much. He had left the base camp with his pack and a light sleeping bag–telling his hunting companions that he'd be back the next day.

They knew he preferred to hunt alone, so they merely grunted as he headed west toward the higher peak. He had scoped a nice ram and desperately wanted it.

Turning his head without thought caused a second searing pain to envelope his being before easing. The movement made him pant like a dog.

Yeah, I remember now, I had him right where I wanted him a single shot sent him toppling to the lower ledge where I could reach him with ease, and what a beaut! A record for sure.

Then a memory out of a nightmare hit Grady with as much force as the actual onslaught. A wolf landed on him like a train and seemed to rip his throat out. Unable to resist, he moved his hand to his throat with much pain–but less than moments earlier–only to feel his throat still intact.

"No . . . " Grady sat up and nearly fell over as gray fog swirled around until black and white sparkles eventually resolved to show he was in a bed inside a small, dark cabin.

"Don't move too swiftly there. I don't like to wash the bedding more than I have to. You'll be spewing your guts out if your not careful."

Grady looked at the man blearily as he wondered where the heck he was.

The guy grinned, showing surprisingly clean, white teeth for a mountain man. "Names Bucky, Samuel Buckingham as christened by my mother and gaining the surname from my father, may his soul never rest in peace." He made his way over to the cot and gingerly shook hands with Grady.

***

"So let me get this straight," Grady implored as he sat at the table a few days later. "I am free to go–but you say I won't like what I see in the city?"

Bucky smiled and hung his tongue out the side of his face a moment before replying, "Yup, that's the way I see it. Scared the bejeezuz out of me, so I hightailed it to the mountains right quick. Like I said day before, ain't like nothing you've ever seen in your life, and the full moon is nice. I mean real nice . . . but it don't make you what you already are." Holding up his hand to stop an argument they had already been over, he restated his view–expecting no back talk. " If you hadn't a shot my sheep I would never have attacked. But you did, and I did, and now you are one of us."

A surprisingly deep growl escaped from Grady, along with a gesture of anger; nearly breaking the table into two pieces as he slammed his fist down.

"Fine, I believe you. Shoot, I have to. I've seen you switch– and I switched in response. Gah, what a sickening feeling! Does it get any better?"

"Been going back and forth now for 80 years, son. Yeah, I s'pose it's easier. Now I hear those choppers a searching for you so we may as well go on out and light that fire."

***

Back in the city Grady immediately felt the difference. His sense of smell was heightened, rarely a good thing. Telling about his time in the woods wasn't too hard he'd told whoppers before; he'd fallen off a ledge, got knocked out and lost his memory for a few days, and came to with Bucky taking care of him. No problems there. The lean hunter was known for his daring adventures in the wilds of nature.

But what he was not prepared for, even though Bucky tried to warn him, was the vast variety of things never before seen. Going to work was eye opening, Grady nearly ran his truck off the road as he saw crowds, yes, literally crowds of people on the sidewalks–and even in the middle of the road–dressed in all styles and periods of clothing. He checked his watch to ensure he had his dates correct. Yes, it was Oct. 29th, not yet Halloween.

Inside the federal building for work was worse. At the check point, he did a double take. He felt sure his golden-green eyes were bugging out of his head at the sight before him.

"What the . . . ?" he began, as the hair on his neck began to rise. Fighting the urge to transition, he breathed deeply and grimaced at the stench brought to his nose by the deep inhalation.

Henry, Good Old Henry, the one who checked him in every morning was not his normal self. Yes, he was in uniform, and his messy white hair still went in every direction, but his skin was gray and his eyes gleamed silvery-green. The folds of his flesh drooped deeply from his jowl, and from his wet lips hung a long viscous string of saliva–dangling precariously, catching Grady's attention. At the same time, this "new" Henry's own eyes narrowed in recognition of Grady's transformation.

"Mr. Parson. Care for an escort today?"

Eyes widened in fear, Grady looked inside only to see the place teeming with hideous creatures far worse than Good Old Henry. Nodding weakly, he acquiesced.

Once inside his private office, Grady asked, "It's like this all the time?"

A long strand of slimy spittle fell from Henry's lip as he sucked the rest back in, swallowed noisily, and then replied.

"Pretty much . . . eh, it's a little more busy as we prepare for Halloween. It will be a madhouse, mmm and I advise you not to come to work until November 2nd."

"Hold up, who are you to advise me? I'm an especially important guy around here, remember?" He held his hands up and pointed his sharp nose at all the trappings of his fancy office.

Henry shook his head with a chuckle and replied, "Game has changed, sir. Oh, you are still required to do your regular job, but Werewolves fall under my purview, along with Ogres, Trolls, and Dopplegangers."

"Dopple what?"

Henry went to the computer, typed in a security code, and pulled up a file on supernatural species. "Read up and call me when you have a question. Someone will be in to debrief you shortly–we keep records of each transformation."

***

October 31st. Grady woke with a start. Something went flitting through his room, then a three foot tall creature crawled out from beneath his bed and scurried out the door.

Unable to control his reaction, he transformed into his new natural state–gray fur raised as his hackles attested to the fear and anger he felt. After chasing the creature down the stairs, he quickly caught it with a satisfying crunch, breaking it's legs. Swiftly his desire overcame any sanity harbored deep within as he ate the Goblin's soft entrails.

Laughter and cheering accompanied the death. Once his anger had cooled, the wolf looked up to see various Sprites and Fairies swinging on the chandelier. Only they were not the normal Fairies he had been seeing the last few days. These were dark, very dark.

In disgust, the wolf flung the broken, disemboweled body away from him and eased back into his Human form. The Sprites called out sounds of disappointment until they noticed he was no longer clothed and changed their booing to jeers, whistles, and catcalls.

"Out! Out I say. I didn't invite you here, now leave!"

They howled in delight and stayed right where they were.

A deep growl escaped from his broad chest, Grady then muttered, "I knew I should'nt have skimmed over that section on house guests."

From between his house plants, a sweet little Fairy poked her head out and said, "Easy enough to fix, ye just need wards placed on every opening."

With a sigh Grady wrapped the small blanket sitting on the couch around his waist and plopped down, "And where, pray tell, do I find such a being to provide this service – and at what price?"

The Fairy flitted out of hiding and into the room. Her blue Fairy dust spilled enchantingly, causing Grady's anger and shame to ease up. Yet glancing at the carnage and blood brought it right back. He felt oafish and hideous in contrast to her magical beauty. *I'm every bit as disgusting as Henry the Troll, Good Old Henry.*

Winging closer, she landed on his shoulder and soothed his fears with her touch.

"Now, none of this melancholy, love. It's Halloween!"

His eyes went wide at the thought that this was something to be glad about; from what he had been reading Halloween was the day when the flood gates opened and all spirits past, present, and future could roam the earth freely–that did not sound good.

Musical laughter chimed as the sweet Fairy appeared to read his thoughts, "Aye 'tis a glorious day of dancing and good cheer. But let's do stay on topic."

She raised her impish face up to the dark Fairies still swinging from the light fixtures. "Me own uncle is a master weaver of spells, and his price is small. But he is busy, so I can do it for a smaller price."

Grady admired the features of the wee fae, she wore a gossamer wisp of cloth clinging strategically to her form of its own accord.

Sensing his approval, she laughed again and flew around his head twice. She then flitted through the house creating wards of protection. Lastly, with a grand incantation she expelled the unruly Sprites.

***

Grady returned to his room after having worked out a deal with Sienna. Oddest request ever, but what she wanted was permission to collect fur from the werewolf's coat–for a year. The Blue Fairy said she was going to weave it into fabulous blankets which would fetch wealth and fame. What wealth a Fairy needed Grady had not yet divined since a Fairy could conjure up most anything it needed.

Sienna told Grady about the portals beneath the beds– Goblins use them to scare children and to come out at night. On Halloween, Goblins are apt to spew out of them all day. But she, Sienna, opined that having killed the first, is was safe to assume the rest were hesitant. Looking beneath the bed it appeared normal, and then a glimmer showed a slight difference indicating where the portal was. In a calm but compelling voice, Grady said, "If any of you want the same fate show your face now. Otherwise begone and leave me be."

Chuckling in near hysteria, he flopped on his bed as he recalled his mother teaching him that very phrase when he was five years old complaining about noises beneath his bed.

His mother had shone a flashlight under the bed telling him that the light killed the Goblins and Beasties of the night. She told him all he had to do was flash the light and say those same words and he would sleep in peace.

Funny thing is, he was sure he had heard noises, but could never convince her, and yet the light and chant had worked. He used it until he was ten.

With a growl of anguish, the past two nights returned to his memory; the moon had risen full on the 29th and continued full last night as well. The feeling that came over him as the moon rose was one he felt unable to describe.

Having gone into the backyard, his eyes went towards the eastern sky where the moon was on the horizon. It made him want to cry; such beauty sang to him.

Then that horrific feeling as his body changed. Only this time it was not truly horrific–more fierce, frenzied, needed. It was a sensual experience as the moon called out to him as strongly as any lover ever had. Still, Bucky assured him he need never lose all control, thus rather than run into the city where people were, as much as he desired snapping his jaws on some tasty morsel, he ran towards the woods behind his house and up the small hill to enjoy the moon alone.

To howl with such freedom had never seemed like anything that would cause as much joy as it did, but now, laying on his bed, Grady concluded it was indeed worth being transformed for that experience alone. The thought of hunting, without his gun, was pretty exciting as well. So that is what he did. First the stinking neighbors' dog, which he had told the guy to keep locked up on several occasions, and then deer, rabbits, and anything that moved there in the woods.

With a sigh, he said aloud, "Yep, Bucky old boy, I understand now why you live in the woods."

The fear of losing control among regular people was there but tempered by the fact that he knew he was under surveillance. Henry was a member of the Elite Paranormal Squad, and Grady had learned that Beasties of every hue did indeed exist, but there were laws in place and armies of good supernaturals working hard to keep the smaller numbers of those choosing evil in check. So at the moment, Grady was on probation. If he passed he would be initiated into the guard–mainly due to his government position. But also because Werewolves were rare and highly useful.

With a snort he went to shower, having been in the woods the past two days he was definitely in need. Recalling another conversation with Henry he soaped up.

"So tell me this, if Werewolves are so sought after, why don't you just create more?"

The Troll shook his head splattering slime on the desk and papers sitting there. "Son, you didn't read the reports I gave you very well. We have laws . . . it's against the law to create beings without consent . . . and it's against the law to reveal supernatural anything to regular people so that effectively limits the number of new creatures. We know about Bucky and leave him be, he wants nothing to do with the Squad but neither does he seek to thwart the system.

"We get a new Werewolf maybe once or twice a year the world over. You make number two for 2012. Fact is, you can't give birth to Werewolves, not by mating with a wolf in full wolf form, and not by having relations with a human. Only the bite from a wolf-man in transition causes another to transform, and yes that includes animals. Trust me, we've seen some weird creations, but they generally get taken out pretty fast."

Grady thought it over and then asked, "So why are we so highly prized?"

The Troll coughed up some wet, rattly phlegm and replied, "Thought you'd never ask. That was not in your report because those files are only seen by supernaturals with access, and not every one knows the truth. Fact is wolves–all canines, actually– can see spirits, the essence of beings on another plane of existence. What people call ghosts and angels."

"Yeah! I see them. You mean you can't?"

Henry replied in the negative.

Grady couldn't remember if he had shampooed so he went through the motions and then added conditioner as he pondered what kind of assignments he would have regarding his special skills.

***

Sienna convincingly coaxed Grady into joining her in the Halloween, or rather Samhain, celebrations. She told him they would be attended by all members of the Fair Realms and those who were Fell as well. Having transformed herself to full human stature, Grady hoped to better see how her clothes connected, or not to her form. But as she transitioned she clothed herself in a stunning witches costume circa 1500's era. Black and deep blue silk swished seductively, and her tiny waist was cinched tightly with a corset trimmed in deep red ruffles along the top.

Unable to resist, Grady let out a wolfy howl which caused Sienna's eyes to widen even as she blushed and smiled.

"Ha, I have never spent the evening with a Werewolf, but I think this is going to be fun."

Leading the way out the back door and into the woods, Sienna guided Grady towards a huge bonfire, which sat in a clearing that Grady knew for certain did not exist in his woods.

They passed through several sparkly portals notably guarded by ghostly sentinels. The urge to ask if Sienna could see them was strong but he resisted. Instead, he noted her small hand signals and a return nod or finger twitch in reply.

Just my luck, he thought. *Finally find a girl with the hots for me, and she's probably the subject of an investigation. Like the last two . . .*

Warily he looked about the crowd, Henry was there but stayed with the other Trolls. Goblins were dancing merrily with their floppy ears bouncing about causing laughter among those stopping to watch. The music was provided by any and all who wished to play–and it appeared half the group did indeed wish. Grady quickly pushed aside any fleeting guilt over having eaten a Goblin. The killing part didn't bother him one bit. Had the Goblin appeared in his sight any other day before his transformation it would be just as dead–the gun on the nightstand assured that outcome.

Soon, Grady let go of his inhibitions and danced about the fire with Sienna and countless other Fairies, Elves, and even a female Goblin or two. Still, as midnight approached he felt an apprehension as the portals between the living and the dead opened ever wider. The crowd was astounding, nearly overwhelming.

Pulling away from the fire, he found himself sitting alone on a rock. The moon should have been waning, but feeling it's pull he saw it was indeed still one hundred percent full. Fearing to transform before hundreds he sought to move further away when a voice he recognized stopped him in his tracks.

"Stay."

Turning, he saw the filmy image of his grandmother. As he stared in wonder, she became solid and youthful.

"Grady, I am so proud of you."

He feared to reach for her and yet longed to, his love for her was more than it was for his mother, unfairly or not. She had raised him.

Reaching out, she said, "Yes, on this night we can touch." Then she embraced him and continued, "Go ahead and transform, these are your friends. You can trust them."

It felt so wrong. She was an angel, Werewolves were evil, weren't they? Still, the mystically full moon pulled stronger, and he heard his fellow Werewolves whom he had yet to meet, already howling.

Unable to stave it off any longer he gave in to the primal urge to worship the moon fully, with everything he had.

He enjoyed the stretching of each muscle as his back tightened in such a way to cause him to arch back tighter which improved his view of the moon. Sweet sensations of pleasure coursed through his body as if truly Diana blessed him with her love. To howl at the moon never seemed more right.

Letting go completely, he forgot all pretense and concern. Now, fully willing to experience the night as one would expect, singing in harmony and counter melodies throughout the night, Grady felt at one with himself, his brothers, and the moon.

Chapter 10

Arianna's Trying Afternoon

My visitor was a skittish Brownie. I could understand his fear, going into the depths themselves are not frightful, and certainly not for Brownies it is home to that species just as much as it is to my Goblin Clan; but the portal chosen, MY portal, leads to our dear and yet frightful King. Coaxing a story out of him took quite a bit of time and energy. I must say I have never had to try as hard as I did. But once he revealed that he worked in the Fair Realms High Queen's own Castle, I understood all the more reason for his hesitancy. Yet I redoubled my efforts as I desired a story about the Royal family.

I assume he felt this little tale about the youngest daughter was most benign. I am grateful for it. For being such a simple story it brought me a peace I did not know I needed.

Life is what it is and we must relish what we have.

Arianna had had her limit of being told what to do.

Making her way resolutely into her mother's chamber she plopped down on the dais at her mother's feet. Queen Gwenarra looked patiently down at her youngest and most trying daughter—without a word.

Arianna wanted to be acknowledged, so she refused to say anything either. She huffed. She flopped her hands lazily on the step, she tapped her feet simultaneously—and singly. She glanced up at her mother with a spiteful glare, while still managing to keep it respectful.

Gwenarra rolled her eyes and finally said, "I see you, daughter. What is it that you desire?"

Now Arianna felt like bottling up and not saying what was on her mind. She hated that she felt this way and didn't know how to express herself. She sighed and then stood up to face her mother sitting upon the Crystal Throne.

"Mother, I am simply frustrated with my sisters, the trees, and even the stream in the woods!"

Do keep in mind that Arianna was an Elvin Princess and that her mother was Queen of all the Magical Realms. The Princess Arianna had been trying to use her powers of shaping and was frustrated because she didn't have enough influence to get the trees to bend as she desired, nor would the stream sing the songs she sent their way . . . and well, as far as her sisters . . . being the youngest meant Arianna would never have any kind of control over their actions.

Gwennara's soft golden curls cascaded to her waist in ringlets. Her pale skin and clear blue eyes were reflected in her daughter who looked nearly identical. The queen's eyes crinkled as she smiled and replied, "Life is like an apple, eat it."

She then bowed her head in dismissal; when Arianna failed to leave she flicked her wrist gracefully as if shooing a fly.

Arianna lowered her gaze, curtsied with grace, and departed.

How was that an answer to her trials?

She made her way through the back gardens, past the roses, and then the orchard until she came to the deep green woods beyond the proper yard. Trees made her feel so safe, so loved, and welcomed. She felt a connection to the trees and this was why it upset her so much that they refused to accept her desire to alter them . . . she stopped and thought about that.

Sitting down among the ferns she pondered . . . *I love the trees and yet I wished to change them. Is that fair of me? They are what they are and have no need of my interference. Life is like an apple, eat it.*

Then out loud she said, "Oh Mother! How wise you are . . . life is what it is. Like an apple it simply is; and what are apples good for?? Eating!"

She sang out to the Dryads who tended the trees, "Forgive my interference; do carry on." And then to herself she said, "Life is for living and that is what we shall do."

The brook burbled in agreement.

Chapter 11

The Doctor's Monologue

Ah, now this tale is intriguing. It stems from an age long before my birth. Before the birth of my King and all living beings upon the earth as far as I know. It is possible a Dragon or two remain from that time. It happened before the flood of the world. Of that era, I have read tales of what it was like down below, to have all the rivers flow to the surface as they did. It was a fascinating event for earthdwellers to be sure. My visitor happened to be a historian on a quest for books and stories of that period. The flood in particular, but also from the years before, when Humans had risen to their pinnacle before destroying all that they had gained. They tend to do that, repeatedly . . .

I envied the historian as he descended to visit the vast Library of Cormach, a place where much of my youth was spent. I see that my father was indeed kind to send me here where I have a small degree of what resides in that sanctuary. At any rate, this story tells about the stimulus that led to the great uprising—which eventually brought about Humanities' fall. I hear tell similar things are on the horizon once again.

Potential is more important than knowledge.

That was his slogan.

They all bought into it, everyone of them. He promised great potential for all.

I was just a kid back then, ten years old. I had no concern for politics. Mom and Dad seemed to think that Mr. Absalom was a very fine man. They put his little posters in the lawn . . . making it hard to play tag with my friends.

Well he won the election, repeatedly. He promised potential, and from the start he made it possible for all to get the free medical care they had demanded for years. Thing is, what they didn't know didn't hurt them. That became a silent policy, one fostered on a need to know basis.

I grew up to become a doctor. Being one who needed to know, I now do. Yet the government paid for my fine education, another free benefit afforded by his eminent beneficence. Of course, the price for such bounty is one's servitude . . . never would they call it slavery.

No, slavery we were taught, was stealing people from their homes and forcing them to live in shacks and work endless hours unpaid and barely fed. That is nothing at all like what has happened here, well not just here, pretty much world-wide. The system became accepted almost universally and simultaneously.

Having gained an education it was only reasonable that one devote an equal number of years giving back to society as one had received in education. At first it was just college years. Legislators moved it back to include high school and now it is from preschool until graduate school. After all, they provided free breakfast and lunches, free health care and the finest education money from the government could buy. And so we serve.

Efficiency is key.

That was a new slogan begun twenty years ago. Homes were designed with economy of resources and the most energy efficient designs possible. Obviously, the populace could not argue with such noble desires. New neighborhoods were built with three designs and *six* colors, since our beloved government recognized the need for individuality. Those in high positions within the governmental body, as well as the newly formed News Administers Office, scoffed at the negative comments which said we were being stifled. Not at all, they countered, we were granted freedom from having to ever be in search of the bigger and better things in life. Attitudes fostered in the past were altered, no more was it acceptable to be better than the neighbors. Competition is for sports, not life. Less choices equal greater freedom . . . no need to spend valuable time and energy on superfluous pursuits.

Now they are tearing down old homes, historic homes. It's only fair that we all share equally in the same joy and concern for the planet. We need never have one person above another they said. Except, of course, for they who oversee the needs of the people. Surely we could see the need to respect them for their sacrifice? Willingly, they leave their home-towns and extended family for the sheer pleasure of fulfilling their public duty. To offer us, the people of this great nation, the benefit of their wisdom. Surely they deserve such a small thing as distinctive homes, right?

So now here we are. I am an old man, seventy years old, in fact. I know my fate . . . being a doctor as I have said. I have learned what my potential is, knowledge is power and the masses have been denied knowledge. This I know . . . doctors have been instructed to reduce (and even stop) treatments for those who have no further usefulness to society.

The malls, and parks, and public places appear so very healthy and our productivity as a nation is high. All because we doctors have ceased our heroic efforts to save lives at all cost. Of course, we give the appearance of effort. Infant mortality is at an all time high in equal proportion to the drastic reduction of mental patients and handicapped persons of every kind. Indeed, my children barely recall having seen wheelchairs and my grandchildren do not even know such a thing existed.

Utopia is within our grasp!

Another slogan I saw just last year, before they took away my driving privileges. A big deal is made about getting on in years. I am as fit as I ever was, and yet I am not allowed to take a stroll beyond my driveway to collect the mail.

Hospice care centers have increased in number, they provide many jobs. Such a sweet and noble sacrifice the government has granted to every major city. All people are "allowed" to move in at the age of seventy and are required at the age of seventy-two. It is such a kind thing to vacate our homes to allow the next generation their opportunities to contribute to society. Such a beautiful plan, no one dared find fault with it. Not when it became forcible by law.

Due to a higher influx of death among the greater population, crematoriums have replaced mortuaries completely. My grandchildren are appalled at the very thought of cemeteries and bodies being left in the ground. To visit the place with flowers is archaic . . . and yet, not too far off from what is now done with the dead loved ones.

Even when I was a child it had become quite popular to keep the ashes of a loved one in the home or scattered in one's rose garden. Now, they incorporate the ashes into the clay as well as the glaze. Master potters craft lovely urns, no they call them vases. The vases are taken home and flowers are placed within them. For a year or two anyway.

So yes, I can most assuredly attest I have learned my potential, and for those who have been kept in innocence it is safe to say that ignorance is bliss.

They now say:

Hope is more important than knowledge.

What hope have I?

I am too old to seek for hope, so I will stay with the first slogan. I know my potential and that is to be made into an ashtray. No one lives beyond seventy-two, this is a known fact among the elite within my field. But here is the truth: *Knowledge is power.*

In those sterile hospice centers let me admit, videos are made and conversations recorded to be sent at intervals for years to the loved ones. Random dates are chosen for death dates, family members who have been forbidden to visit are informed and a lovely memorial service is provided, free, of course, from our loving government. No one questions such actions anymore, parents are sent away and then they die. People are freed from the burdens of times past.

Ashes to ashes and something to dust . . .

Epilogue

The Doctor's Monologue was distributed among the underground resistance. It took years but eventually the old began to act out. No longer did they go peacefully into the hospice care centers . . . soon it became part of the police squad's duties to collect the aged.

A shift was felt.

Utopia's peace was shattered.

Chapter 12

𝒮𝒽𝒶𝒹𝑜𝓌 𝒟𝒶𝓃𝒸𝑒𝓇𝓈

At times I grow weary of the shadows in the Arcadium. Especially in winter when the sun no longer sends her rays through the stained glass storefront. It makes me feel a degree of pleasure to think that by lighting the interior I am then sharing the beauty of those works of art with passersby on the street.

One such soul felt drawn to enter. After asking about the manner of business that I participate in, he noticed the portal. And I thought him a mere human! Turned out he was what he termed a Shadowmancer. He speaks for shadows, interprets them, and he even owns his own little curiosity shop wherein he buys and sells shadows. Who knew such a thing existed among mankind? Not I. It is new, surely, for I have never read of such things in my many years, centuries, spent as Portal Master. He did not wish to pass through the portal, just a small look inside. This is his tale, a story as told to him by shadows.

Voiceless, we watch.

He woke up and padded to the bathroom . . .
the normal routine ensued. His preference for the dark was
pleasing to our sensibilities. In the dark we stretch out and
mingle . . . more than one, we enjoy sociality, unlike that
which is granted within the light.

Making his way to the bright kitchen, we hid within the
shadows, beneath his being is generally safe.

To play along opposite the light is what we do, what we
know.

Dancers of shadow we love the light, for without it we
cannot dance.

Leaving his home we played beside him, dark and
crisp in the bright morning rays. He turned towards the office
building where he worked. Causing us to dance before him.
We loved being able to see his beautiful face, one we knew so
well. So coveted. We yearned to have features we knew we
could never have. His eyes were deep, hooded . . . our very
shadows lived in the crevices there. A golden gleam existed
within the brown of his eyes, lighting his face. His nose was
straight and fine, his hair short and easily blown about by the
wind. Such joy for us; we danced with the breeze. His ears
stick out giving our shape distinction when the lighting is
right.

Did we mention how we love the light?

He stepped inside, greeting his secretary and went to his office.

Our singular existence was disturbed when two men with dull black weapons entered the room, dragging the secretary and one other into the office, where we sat beneath the desk mingling as shadows do.

Though we have no auditory sensations, knowledge is transferred, we know of speech and sound. We know not how we know, but we do.

Dread entered with the shadows of those men. Dark and foul they were not like us. The woman was thrown onto the desk; her shadows mingled with ours. Fright and wonderment played about. We shored her dancers up and they rallied to maintain their connection to her.

Time played on, and on. A scuffle ensued and the foul weapon fired into the man . . . that other whom we had never met. His shadows stayed beneath him for a moment, yet we felt their diminished hope seep into the air. Never had we seen the transfer of dancers in such a fiendish manner . . . for as the shadows fled his dying body, those from the man who had fired his weapon took their place beneath the tenement of clay . . . sickeningly, we felt their joy at being attached to the corpse.

Shadow dancers mourned, as they, the hellish dark ones, neared our home. Many leapt upon us; fierce and ugly was the dance . . . no, not a dance at all. Savage and brutal they sought to disengage us from our only habitation!

Our beautiful host collapsed, having been hit with the dark non-gleaming gun. The woman huddled nearby, grasping at the body of our person, running her hands across his smooth brow. Sorrow engulfed the darkness of our existence.

Still, we battled. We would have none of this darker frightful dancing in our midst. Hours passed and the light within the office remained constant. A diffused light, which hardly gave us purchase.

He roused, our person, and we silently expressed our joy. The eased dread of having need to flee refreshed our resolve, and we battled once more against they who sought to lay claim upon our home.

But they would not leave. Those shadows caught hold and became one with us. The men with the guns left the room and never returned. We went with our host as he rode within a vehicle to a hospital, a place filled with shadows of every flavor and emotion. Frightful, we had only been there once before, at our birth, even then it had been frightful . . . for we had been new.

We returned home, our host and our new darker shadow dancers. Our joy diminished and never did we gain again the innocence of our prior experience. Our previous happiness was colored by that day.

We dance in the shadows. Voiceless.

Chapter 13

The Bitter End

Just when I was dwelling in dark thoughts and self-pity, a guest came along who was one unnamed but prominent writer from the late 1900s. Turns out he's an Elf. He enjoyed Dream hopping quite a bit and in one particular life he sampled he was quite the daredevil. He's a natural bard so I cannot say whether this is a true tale as experienced in an alternate life, or whether he made it up on the fly, so to speak.

Either way he brought me out of my doldrums and gave me a good laugh. After he passed through the portal I even felt like reading a few of his books, a good storyteller can do that to a fella. I found out later he chose to stay out of the world, allowing his Human fans to believe the news reports. But I so happen to know that he spends a good portion of his time visiting someone in the caverns below. The rest of his time is spent in the Land of Eternal Spring, still writing and sharing his gifts with new fans. And let's not blame the boa constrictor!

It's a curious thing really. To be conscious and unable to move. I've no one but myself to "speak" to, as my mouth cannot even respond. But I have this curious need to narrate my demise. Being a storyteller I would dearly love to explain my situation.

I was on holiday. A small cruise line promised a more tailored and unique experience. I enjoyed visiting one island after the other, noting the similarities and differences was fascinating. Indeed, someone may find my journal and wonder whatever happened to me.

gasp It's starting.

So as it happened. The small boat we used for day trips capsized when a rogue wave came up from the sea. I spent a day and a half floating in a piece of the broken hull.

I and one other washed ashore, not far from each other. Together we determined a need to build a shelter. The next day as we were attempting to find food, we noted a village. Such joy!

Making our way there, we were met by men dressed much like all the other islanders we had met, if a bit more crude and unwashed.

Yet we were welcomed with cheers and chants. Fed wonderfully for a week. And then it happened.

Oh, gee

I must finish my tale. Even if it is for me and none else. What, you might ask, happened?

Good question and I shall tell you. We were bathed and prepared for a feast as though we were honored guests. I was surprised they even had tubs, as I had previously mentioned, they are a rather filthy lot. And may I now add loathsome?

An ornate goblet was brought forth. Custom has been that we as honored guests drink so as not to offend. Often the drinks are nasty, pure and simple. Yet, most induce euphoria.

This was no different, I was tempted to spit it out, but refrained. Would that I had!

Oh my

We passed out. When I came to I was in my current state. My companion is lying beside me. His face is directly in my line of sight. Such a hideous end . . . one I would never wish upon my worst enemy. Nope, not even Sadie. We are each able to move our eyes. To view each other's state of being. Meanwhile, chanting is all around us, an occasional laugh from a child or a quick scolding of a parent can be heard. The sea gulls' squawk. The soft shushing of the waves give a surreal quality to it all.

Oh fiddle

I can feel my breathing increase. I think some of my feeling is returning. The eyes of my companion, John—let's name him, a man should never leave this world unnamed, John Hampton from Middlesex. John's eyes have widened in terror; I am sure mine mirror his. The torture! Yes, I can feel a burning in my toes, would that I had drunk more!

Oh heck

Drums and clapping have been added. A frenzied tempo greets my ears. I do believe I may pass out. I can look no more. Goodbye, John. Please rehearse my name. That is all I can hope for now.

Oh, dread

Even now it's not over, but it hurts. Ah, the burning! Hell was never described thus.

My last thought is that this surely counts as penance. I pray the Lord my soul to take . . .

Chapter 14

Jantal's Quest

The adventuring spirit within me lies dormant most days. The stories I collect fill me with enough food for thought to last me, often for months at a time. I must confess, I did happen to go a questing once or twice myself before this assignment was placed upon my shoulders. I have learned that more often than not such journeys fall into three categories: One for glory—simply put, to truly be a hero. Two for love; and lastly out of obligation and true altruism. This story came to me from Merlin himself. Now that one is a mystery worth studying if you can get a story about him, be that as it may, he came by and shared this fine tale about a youth sent by custom on a journey. He went out of obligation and returned a hero.

I do wish my own quest had as much success. Still I carry fond memories of one in particular with whom I would have found comfort in, had my life gone in another direction. Having gained a poets heart I can now say that perhaps the desire to love and be loved is stronger and more glorious than the actual doing. The thoughts and ideals keep a person going—alas, my thoughts have wandered from the tale at hand. Thinking about going on a quest does that to me . .

Please lets forget about me, Jantal is a fine young man, learn of him, find the integrity he displays. His power lies within his character.

Jantal pondered his dilemma.

His Quest was meant to be hard, but he had never even imagined such a thing could be done. This was the assignment he had drawn:

Visit the underworld and bring back the Questing Stone of Alandria.

That's what was written on the slip of paper he had drawn from The Cup of Rigors.

At eighteen, and being the son of the Council Chief, he was expected to be the leader of the expedition of youths. He was taller and broader, but essentially they looked similar, almost everyone had black hair. The rare redhead or brunette made an appearance in the village, but not often.

Four other boys had birthdays that cycle. This did not include Hansi his birthday was the cycle before and his other best friend,   Jobacci had his birthday one day later—in the new cycle. Not having his friends with him and with the added pressure of being leader was getting the best of him.

Despite his inner turmoil and doubts, Jantal tried to be positive in front of his cycle mates. Sighing, he stood and called the break over, "Up we go guys, let's find the Curtain of Aliandara."

Kale chuckled, "You know it's interesting how similar those two names are. Alandria and Aliandara? Do you think there is a connection?"

Jantal shrugged but thought it over as he led the troupe through the tall grass. They had left their small mountain village a week gone by. Home was green and filled with trees and small clearings for crops. Now they were on the Plain of Gercion, Tromanjia. Gypsies roamed the plains in their wagons and on their fine stallions. Jantal had hoped for a Quest to live among the Tromanjia, like Dar, his brother. Dar came home with a bride. She was now with child for the second time and still as beautiful as ever.

Aliandara was an ancient legendary heroine, daughter of He Who Sits on High. It was said that when she was banished from the high mountain home, she turned to weeping so strenuously that the rivers of the world were added upon, causing them to spill over the sides of the world. Those falls became curtains of water. Some had names, others had been long forgotten as most people preferred not to live so close to the edge.

Jantal had been given an old map which so far had been correct. They were nearing the edge already. It gave him a queasy feeling, he even felt unsteady. In the distance, he looked and saw the end of the world. Still, it was another hour before they were actually–there.

So, Alandria. Name of our mountain home. Legends say Alandria was a visitor from the underworld. One day she set out on her own Quest, it is said that women were the ones to Quest down below. She arrived upon the surface and liked what she found, she traveled far and wide and settled in the cool green and blue mountains closer to the Throne of He Who Sits on High. Having found a mate, she soon populated the small village and is now honored as the mother of our Clan. Jantal thought about how many years had passed, it had been over a thousand, or so the records declared.

Everyone knew that story, it was told yearly on the night

of Her Festival of Naming. But what intrigued Jantal about Kale's question was, that Jantal knew another story. One told only to the Council Chiefs sons.

Jantal rehearsed part of the tale to himself. *It is said that Aliandara had visited the underworld, having swam down her river of tears. The Curtain of Aliandara was so named because it was the path she took. Once there, she stayed after having found happiness and relief from her loneliness and sorrow. Taking a husband, she then had many children. One daughter she named Alandria and then she sent her on a Quest. So yes, they certainly had a connection.* Was he supposed to keep that secret? Jantal did not know.

They heard the river and the falls before they saw it. Climbing a rise, leaving the tall grass behind, they stopped and stood reaching out to one another as vertigo took hold. Eventually, they fell to their knees. Had they not feared falling it would have been out of reverence.

The river was broad and deep. The sound was louder than any mountain fall they had near their home. The mist caught several rainbows as the sun settled near the horizon directly behind them.

Jantal would have liked to have said, "Set up camp." But it was several hours before true dark would be upon them. Taking out the map he spread it on the ground for all to see.

"So how many should go over?" he asked, looking from one newly-made man to the next.

Kale swallowed and looked at the map. Thrasher and his twin Swat looked at each other and grinned. It was no secret that they wanted to go over the falls. Jantal obviously had to go as he was entrusted with securing the stone.

"Okay. Kale and Bush, you two stay here and set up camp." Using the generic term for the twins, he said, "Boys, you are coming with me."

With a whoop, they fell in line. They crept to the edge, eventually crawling on their bellies as fear of falling took over again. It seemed silly to Jantal; as mountain folk, they were used to climbing cliffs and jumping casually over chasm hundreds of feet deep. But this felt different.

Jantal felt awed even as the twins each issued a near silent exhalation. Looking over the edge, they saw nothing but raw dirt with rocks and roots jutting out here and there.

Then they saw it, a seemingly man-made stairway leading directly under the falls. Jantal let out a sigh of relief, as he had feared they would have to ride the falls down—no telling how that would have gone. He shuddered to think on it now.

Still, the stairs were quite narrow. He opted to attach a rope as he made his way down. The twins followed suit; putting on their harnesses and joking about who was more clumsy.

Getting to the stairs was a bit tricky, but once over the edge, they found that gravity actually kind of pushed them fairly close to the side, not quite as precarious as a normal cliff. Once beneath the fall they felt an eerie sense of quiet and calm, the noise was so loud they may as well be deaf. The stairway widened halfway down, it became nicer, and they felt as though they were walking perpendicular to the side of the world. After twenty minutes, they realized that they were indeed walking upright as the river flowed beside them soft and quiet now. The stairs had flattened out, becoming farther apart until they were mere stepping stones. They looked back and saw the roiling white water. Grass and moss grew in patches but looking about he saw the plants became fuller further away. Was this the underworld? It really seemed to be the side as he had seen looking over the edge. Jantal felt his head beginning to ache.

It was getting dark. He had failed to take into account the fact that the sun setting above was now blocked from them. The moon was bright though, offering fairly good vision. Again they heard the roar of the river as the water fell off the next edge of the world.

Lighting a torch to ensure their safety, Thrasher crept to the edge. It was easy to see, as a soft orange glow radiated into the sky along the farthest horizon.

"Must be the dawn breaking," Jantal reasoned.

They crept closer but found no edge. It simply rounded into a hill going downward, but not so steep. Standing up they walked cautiously staying near the river. Eventually, they were in full daylight, witnessing a glorious sunrise breaking past spires, which at first they took for trees. Looking closer they beheld a magnificent city before them surrounded by a great barrier of pearlescent white. They saw no gate.

Jantal stopped to have their evening meal. "Well, it would be dinner time were we up above." Thrasher and Swat agreed and set to filling their water bladders.

No sooner had they finished their meal than a section of the seamless wall opened, and a strange horseless wagon came wheeling up to them. Fearing an attack the three near men stood side by side, hands on hilts.

The accent was odd, but they spoke the same language, something Jantal had feared would not be—he only knew

Alandrian and Brendoran fluently. No one tried to speak the Gypsy tongue unless invited.

"Well, well, well. It looks like the old wizard was right. I assume you claim to come from above?"

The man was middle-aged but fit and cunning. At least Jantal saw him that way. He apparently expected them. Whether that was a good thing, Jantal did not yet know. He nodded courteously and replied, "I am Jantal Al-an. I seek the Questing Stone of Alandria."

Men sitting on the back of the wagon chuckled but then hushed at the stern look of the middle-aged man.

"Indeed. It appears you have said the magic words. Lucky for you; we would have had to disarm you and take you to the dungeons. Ah, pardon me. My name is Morrs, Merlin spoke of you. He's been waiting. Decades according to him."

Riding inside the horseless wagon was fascinating. Soon they were within the city walls and transferred to a nicer wagon. Sleek and shiny black. The seats were soft and made of the finest leather Jantal had ever felt.

The world beneath his own was wondrous and filled with technology never even dreamed of. Questions filled his head, but he knew better than to ask these apparent servants.

It was assumed that they were tired. Evidently they knew what time it was up above. The three young Questers were shown to private rooms with personal bathrooms and showers for each of them. A luxury only had in the largest of cities top-side. In their village, only the chiefs had their own bathrooms. Otherwise, each household shared with the one neighboring them. They had always felt superior with their technology as it was better than those in the lower villages over which they ruled.

Jantal was fascinated with knowledge and tinkering. This was like a wonderland for him!

Exhaustion took over, so after donning sleep wear, he fell promptly asleep.

A soft knock woke Jantal. He was informed that Merlin would see him in thirty minutes. He wondered if Merlin was the Chief or the Wizard. Pulling on clean clothes from his pack he assured he looked his best in the mirror.

Jantal had never been overly concerned about his looks, but now he felt shabby. His black hair hung just at eye level in front, then tapered to a point in the middle of his back. He had wrapped his head with the colors of his family. Two narrow ribbons—one blue as the sky, and the other the color of the majestic pines. His eyes were the same blue if a bit cloudy. His skin was tanned from the sun but not overly dark. Certainly not as dark as Tromanjian's were. He had been shocked when he saw how dark his brother's son was, having assumed Gypsies were dark from living on the plains. His musing was interrupted as a young boy came to lead him and the twins down the hall.

Several flights of stairs and many twists and turns had them totally lost. Only then, at that point of complete disorientation, did it seem they were allowed to meet the great Wizard. Merlin had indeed been expecting them.

As it turned out. Merlin was a great-great grandson of Aliandara, and even more telling—brother of Alandria.

"So you see, it was I who took the Questing Stone for safe keeping when my dear sister died. I left a book for your wise ones to read. It told them at what point in their history, their future rather, to send one to return the stone to it's place of honor. I take it electricity has been discovered, and battery operated torches. This is wonderful!"

He beamed so joyously that Jantal could not help but smile back. "So you are saying you were waiting for us to—sort of catch up? Why not simply share your knowledge? Why leave us to learn it on our own?"

"'Twas not your time my dear boy, that's all there is to it. Simply not yet your time."

The old wizard stood and went to a stand. Opening the box which sat there, he revealed that which legend had spoken of. The Questing Stone emanated a soft glow, whiter than white with blue ripples along the edges.

Jantal feared and yet longed to touch it. The wizard nodded.

Taking the stone, attached as it was to a chain, Jantal felt it's power. Yes, this was right. This was good. Smiling, he thanked Merlin and asked, "So now what? Our books do not say how to use the stone, only that it was lost to us and greatly desired."

Merlin smiled and brushed his mustache out of his mouth. "Yes, my dear boy, I know. I wrote the book. Wear the stone at night and answers will come to you in your dreams. Lie down with questions, and you will arise with answers. It is a conduit to He Who Sits on High."

Jantal's black rimmed eyes widened, this was marvelous. "So is this meant for just me, my Clan, or the whole village?"

Nodding his head the wizened old man replied, "Sleep on it, and you shall find your answers." Then with a wave of dismissal, they were sent on their way.

And so it was that Jantal became a man, a prophet and a hero. Long and storied are his adventures, but I have not the time to tell them.

Chapter 15

All is Right in My World

I may be getting myself into quite the sentimental mood as I ponder these next few tales. My father the Goblin King has his faults to be sure. But one thing neither I nor my siblings doubted was the love he had for his wife, Minneola. Such love and devotion became a life's quest (ah that word again!) of mine very early on.

To have a loved one look at me with as much admiration and devotion as that of Minneola upon my father, seemed to be the ideal pursuit. Thus I left my father's realm in search of a treasured companion. I found her and, like the male in the following story, I too feel like I have been betrayed.

I am not at liberty to divulge how I came upon this tale, but I do have permission to share it. The story is presented precisely as it was written, not told. So please refrain from disparaging the tense shifts. My hope for my own happiness in some far off future is comforted in the happy ending this sweet tale offers.

Despite reality dictating that happy endings are rare, I feel compelled to include a tale or two which satisfies that yearning, some call it Human Nature. I, of course, am closely acquainted with beings beyond that narrow viewpoint and can attest love is universal amongst all beings, races, creeds, etc.

She was late and tried to hurry, which she knew was a mistake, clumsy as she was. As she should have known, Serenity tripped stepping up onto the curb, dropping her packages. With remorse, she scrambled out of the way while she watched her grapefruit get squished by the taxi as it rounded the corner.

Surprise replaced her sorrow when a kindly hand offered to help her stand

She was mortified when the businessman knelt and retrieved what he could of her groceries. His suit was obviously designer quality. Serenity frowned when his knees became scuffed with dirt.

"Pity you lost your fruit," he said, handing her the other bag.

Gaining her voice, she answered, "Yes, I was looking forward to that, too. Thank you."

He looked her in the eye. Not something she was used to. "Do take care," he smiled and crossed the street.

Serenity hastened on. More careful, yet still with a good degree of alacrity.

"Mom, I'm back," she called, once she had entered her duplex.

Townhouse really, they were blessed with a patch of green out back, where she spent most of her time. Virginia did get snow, but this year precipitation had been light, so she had spent time out back even in the winter. She had a curious talent for sculpture in many mediums and lately had been obsessed with learning to weld.

Her mother looked at her now, simply shaking her head at her dirty jeans, but then curiosity over whelmed her. "What happened this time?" She sighed with a twinkle in her eye.

Sheepishly Serenity answered, "Nothing, I just misstepped on the corner. I lost a grapefruit, as well as the cherries." She recalled the man, who was most likely the same age as her, his hand hesitant before leaving the spilled cherries in the gutter.

Grace shook her head at her daughter and proceeded to prepare dinner. "Well, the mail is on the table, you have one from the Conservatory."

Serenity tore into the missive; she had been applying at various museums and private art houses requesting her works to be showcased. "They said, 'yes!'"

**

One month later – in late July, Serenity stood in the conservatory speaking with the art director. Her showing was in full swing, people milled about admiring, not only her work but the revered artist Shelle Tarnsworth.

Then she saw him. His smile had never left her thoughts, though she knew it was silly, surely he would not remember her. He was linked arm in arm with Shelle.

Serenity stilled her heart as he strolled near. His glance electrified her. "You clean up well," he said. Serenity had no answer to that, so she simply smiled. Letting go of Shelle, he offered his hand, so Serenity took it. He continued, "Your work is wonderful! I would like to commission you to do a piece for me."

Unable to remain calm, she nearly jumped, yet she recovered before she actually left the ground. Instead, she merely bobbed, still holding his hand. Her blushing caused him to chuckle. They agreed upon a time and date before he left, with Shelle possessively latched onto his arm.

Serenity had made a great debut, the paper gave a lovely glowing review, and she had sold half of her pieces that night. But more than anything, she was excited about her commission by Quarry Hunter. She tried very hard to think of him as Mr. Hunter, but he was so young she could not keep it in her mind, Quarry was such a unique name she found herself saying it out loud when she least expected it.

***

I have to say, she intrigued me that first day when I saw her trip. Her sweet figure, of course, is attractive, but her wavy amber hair reminded me of another, who is lost to me.

My one and only love, Rhiannon had hair like amber, waving gently down her back. Her green eyes had a depth which drew me in. I could get lost in her love for days. So caught up was I in her, that I failed to see she was using me.

It pains me, even now all these centuries later. I had my plans all laid out, most of the northern parts of Europe were to be mine. Shelle uncovered her counter-plot; Rhiannon was working with Baron Downing. I hadn't wanted to believe it.

Rhiannon looked at me that day, her love so evident. "Quarry, you pain me with your accusations. Come, trust me, all will work out for the best." Taking me to our private retreat, she plied her craft delighting me anew. I trusted her so completely.

Shelle and River did not. The pain of finding her body destroyed and ripped to pieces sickens me to even think on it. "My Love! Why?" I had cried out.

Even so, it was too late. She had betrayed me, and my plans were for nothing. We fled to the New World and have been plying our own trade. Never again to have greatness as we had once dreamed of. My passion for the game died with Rhiannon.

This little girl, Serenity, is not she, not my Rhiannon Avonlea. But she is delightful, and I am drawn to her. With all her inept bumbling and lack of grace. I desire to take her under my wing, transform her and – and I know not what will come of it. But I long for that which was lost and see a chance for change in my life.

She, arrived on time, dressed in her cheap cotton shirt and polyester pants. I suppose she had tried to dress up while remaining casual. Jeans would have been better. I myself wore designer jeans artfully ripped and faded. With a casual button up shirt left un-tucked, blue to highlight my eyes.

Her heart sped up, and she blushed so prettily.

I had sent Shelle and River south, to attend a project we had in the works. Shelle was angry, but she knows I do not have feelings for her. I do supersede her in power and authority, so she went, however unwillingly.

We were alone. Just the butler was in attendance, and he was discreet as ever.

"Come along then, I want you to see the room I have in mind for your artwork."

***

Serenity was excited and nervous as she made her way to Quarry's home. It was on the ridge, looking out over the valley. The city sweeping out and away with its grays splashed with color, broken up by greenery. She really did like the city she lived in. Not at all like major cities with very little living greenery. She had been to New York once and liked it about as much as she liked downtown D.C. Only the museums redeem those places, in her mind anyway. Soon she was on the doorstep of the grand mansion.

The doorbell was answered by a graying gentleman who brought her into a receiving room. She sat down on the olive settee. Looking about she tried to get a feel of Quarry's taste, trying to see how her art would fit in. She felt under-dressed in such a refined setting, yet she had wanted to appear casual.

He arrived looking like a model from GQ. His black hair softly swept to the side – without the gel he wore the other two times she had seen him. Her fingers twitched, as the thought to caress his hair flitted through her mind.

He seemed to look right into her soul, quickening her heart; she fought to control her blushing. Yet she blushed easily, so she ignored it and greeted him as gracefully as she could. Bumping his hand before making a connection. He held her hand a moment in both of his as he welcomed her, and then invited her to go deeper into his home.

"This is my conservatory, I should like a series of metal sculptures which reflect my passions." He eyed her once more before smiling and pointing out the plants and piano.

It was an amazing room, one side was like a stage, two steps up where a grand piano sat, off center and solitary. Opposite from the dais was a wall of windows; the walls and islands of seating were decorated with plants, both exotic and common. They sat in pots, large and small on tables and on the floor. The walls themselves were a soft shade of green. The floor was a golden hardwood, which Serenity could not identify.

She began seeing sculptures in her mind's eye. Serenity took a tablet from her bag and asked if she could sketch some ideas.

"Please do." Quarry offered her the choice of the sofa or a chair. She chose the sofa as she was closer to it already.

She felt his body heat as he sat nearby, so that he could see her sketches. Flustered, her hands shook, yet she managed to draw her concepts well enough for him to be impressed.

He seemed as if he was ready to pull her to him at any moment. Serenity began feeling uncomfortable, he was a stranger after all. She shifted, and he smiled congenially as he removed his arm from the back of the sofa.

"You are missing a component in the sculpture." Rising smoothly, he made his way to the piano. "I entertain guests from time to time, as well as host concerts. Music is a passion of mine. Let me play something, which I hope you can create visually."

***

I felt her nervousness; she was not one to be won over so quickly. I would enjoy the challenge.

Making my way to the piano, I felt my own moment of anxiety. The art I wanted would be personal, my love for Rhiannon had never left me, yet it had been put aside. She was gone, and I lived on. Meeting Serenity renewed my feelings of loss, so I wanted something to symbolize that love for Rhiannon, while at the same time allowing me to let go.

I played a gentle song. One evoking a river in its journey to the sea. Gentle and smooth, and then raging and wild, before once again returning to the gentle drift of a widening river as it joins that great body of water, merging seamlessly. My song has words, but I was too overcome with emotions to sing. So I played with as much emotion as I ever have. She was touched, I saw her wipe a tear from her eye. Hanging my head a moment, to collect myself I considered my options.

"Does that tell you more about what I want?" I asked.

She nodded, with a light in her eyes as she watched me return to her. Her breath quickened, my desire grew. Her eyes were green like my true loves. I would be gentle, I determined that I would allow her time. I wrote a check for half the price of the commissioned art. I could not help but smile as her eyes lit up. I am sure she has never earned as much in six months time, if she even has a job.

She agreed to meet with me in a week to discuss how she was progressing. I felt it tortuous to be parted from her, so rather than be far from her, I cloaked my presence with my power and went with her when she left.

She really was inept, it endeared her to me. She nearly ran a red light, slamming on the brakes as she realized she was daydreaming.

"Serenity, what's with you?" she exclaimed out loud.

I willed her to speak her mind, and she did, gratifying my desire.

"Quarry is beyond your league. Even if he thinks you are attractive, he is rich. Beyond rich, he could never care for a girl like you. Look at you dressed as you are." She pursed her lips and snapped the radio on.

Angrily she punched the buttons and then snapped it off

again. She stopped at the bank and then went shopping. To my delight, she bought designer clothes. I prompted her towards those I liked best. She laughed in delight as she modeled in front of the mirror.

"Mom is going to think I have flipped!"

I whispered to her mind, and she bought it anyway; a slinky dress in palest green, a style which I am sure she has never had an opportunity to wear before. I will host an open house and showcase her art once more in my home, the dress will be perfect.

The rest of the week was enlightening, not that I have not viewed the life of mortals many times before, even poor ones like Serenity. No, it was enlightening as I felt my heart reach out to her; she was truly sweet and conscientious. Why I would be drawn to sweetness was a puzzle, but I was. I am.

She had gone to work on the first sculpture the very next day. She really is talented, the price I have paid her will double in the future, I am confident. I will see to it personally. I have decided she will be mine, both heart, and soul.

I chose to pay her a visit the day before we had arranged.

She answered the door with shock registering as she noted my presence on her lowly doorstep.

***

"Mr. Hunter! This is a surprise," she exclaimed. Her cheeks burned dark with shame rather than delight. *What a shame my home is so dreary, she thought.*

"Please, call me Quarry," he said. "I am so excited, I just wanted to see your work in progress. May I?"

Rather than walk him through the house, which smelled of egg salad sandwiches, she led him through the side gate.

In her backyard, she felt calmed and at home as she explained what she was doing and how she felt it would turn out. She had fashioned a trailing ivy with fanciful blossoms in various stages of bloom, from buds to a single petal left. It pulled at his heart despite having just seen it moments before in his hidden state.

She saw his emotion and was gratified that she had captured that which he desired. "So you like it?" she asked, shrugging away her thought that she was asking a redundant question.

His eyes burned with a passion she felt unable to look away from.

"I do. You have a marvelous talent."

He looked away first as she was mesmerized. "Since I have seen your progress, I was wondering, would you care to have dinner with me tomorrow?"

She closed her eyes in shock. The impossible has just occurred. Opening them, she saw his earnest desire so she accepted.

***

With great pleasure I left, only to return in my altered state. I laughed at her innocence as she told her mother and then her friend in detail everything she knew about me. Which was truly limited, even for the persona I was playing, she knew pitifully little. A mother should be more wary of who she allows her daughter to date. But I am good at what I do.

I offered to pick her up, of course. We arrived at an exclusive dining establishment. I kept a room reserved for my sole use. It is over the top, but I was determined. I figured I may as well let her see how powerful I am, in the world of finance, business.

I buy and sell corporations, as well as influence politics. I look young, perhaps twenty-five, though I tell people I am thirty. I have used this particular persona for ten years. Rarely do I meet with an individual more than three times, as far as major transactions are concerned, so it matters not that I do not age. I will be moving on in a few years though, so it is in my best interest to incorporate Serenity into my life soon. She is so sweet that I am unsure she can accept my lifestyle; my true person.

I am not a daemon in the truest sense of the word. I am simply an Immortal stuck on this planet with no way off except through death. A death I do not desire, and so I make my life as entertaining as possible, with games of intrigue. At present we are not in a battle of death, we Immortals I mean. Rhiannon's death was the last, it shocked the other players, even though it affected me the most.

Brutal death done at the hands of my own cousin, River, and one who longs for me, Shelle. I should have dealt with Shelle right then, as I am sure it was her viciousness which defiled my true love's body so violently. But I was in shock and allowed her to guide me through life for a time. As I said, it has been centuries, she no longer suspects that I hold a grudge. River, I forgive; as he ever has my best interest at heart.

Now, as I find my thoughts reaching out to this mortal girl, I fear that which Shelle might do. I know she has this dining room monitored, seeing me with Serenity will draw out her rage. This I am counting on. For this reason, I will be ever so charming with this amber-haired beauty. Shelle cannot dismiss the implications. This is good, as I want her to know she has not been forgiven – when River does that which will end her life.

The room has a low sofa which wraps around the deep mahogany table. The colors are deep and rich. The burgundy carpet and lighter wine colored sofa soak up the muted light, while the mirrored walls splash the light from the chandelier back out again. A balcony and wide windows allow one to see the city lights. I took Serenity out to view the sight before ordering. It had just rained, so the air was fresh and crisp. She shivered; I smoothly wrapped my arms around her. She leaned into me. Recalling Rhiannon doing that very thing caused a lump to form in my throat as I kissed the top of her head. Her heart fluttered, but she controlled it quickly even as she warmed. I imagined her blushing, as I knew she was.

She wore a white dress with a sheer iridescent over-lay. One I had influenced her to buy and wear. Her skin is so flawless and translucent! I revel in her beauty. She could have been a model had she not been so clumsy; well her shyness would be a factor as well. But her looks are such, that when well-dressed, she is stunning.

We reclined on the couch, her eyes taking everything in, so wide and inviting. Dinner delighted her, every course a culinary masterpiece. The serving portions were controlled so that one is sated, not stuffed. A personal request of mine. We discussed childhood memories and high school, college and first jobs. I know Shelle is bored beyond tears, even as she fumes at my flaunting. My other trysts have never been so personal, never have I cared about one's background and life. *Yes,* I smile as I look at Serenity, *Shelle is surely becoming quite agitated.*

"What?" Serenity asks with a smile of her own. She

leans into me.

I adjust our position and take her face into my hands. Searching her face, she looks so very much like my sweet Rhiannon, I can hardly see the difference now. I know not what is happening myself, a tear escapes my eyes and Serenity grows alarmed.

She holds her hand atop mine. "What Quarry? You can tell me."

Steeling myself, I told her that I had been married once. Brokenly, I told how my wife had been brutally murdered. Serenity's compassion overtook her, and she cried with me. Soon we kissed, and we each forgot that which we had been discussing.

True, I have had many opportunities to have women in my life. Never have I shared emotions with them. Serenity stole my heart, and my passion became more than physical. The joy I experienced in that moment was heightened when I felt Shelle's life wink out of existence. River had been true to his word.

All is right in my world.

Chapter 16

Our Lady of the New Dawn

In keeping with my theme of late, this tale was brought to me by my cousin. A true Goblin, unlike me and my siblings, he was not stolen topside and changed into a Goblin. He is the literal son of my father's brother. A Contender for the throne should Father ever step down, or unthinkably worse. . . words I cannot utter nor write. Putting aside such unpleasantness, love continues it's silly pitty-pattering through my mind. My cousin spied upon the home of one Doctor Carlton Dietrich. He managed to chase all the Brownies away and had free range over the entire estate. The estate is such a lovely place. He shared visuals of it with me in my Dreams within the Void.

Sadly, my cousin, Olivar, cannot come into my presence, so he visits me from time to time as I Dream. Having learned of my odd penchant for collecting tales, he offered me this fine gem.

Again, I cannot tell if this is in this world's time-line or another. Olivar was awakened before he finished talking with me and has yet to return. I do hope nothing dire has happened.

Nevertheless, as this story attests, hope remains when all seems lost.

"Annabelle! I need you!" he called frantically.

The young lady rose from where she sat – before a microscope – to see what he wanted. The debonair doctor was heir to the famed creator of the private computationator, or as it soon came to be called, the PC. That was in 1850, Herr Dietrich was commissioned by Prince Albert years before to study the mechanics of fact storing within machines. Huge rooms were built to house the initial creations, then Herr Dietrich discovered the workings of micro-flakes as he termed them. It revolutionized the world, making him wealthy beyond knowing. Now, in 1950, his great-grandson was sole heir and had made a name for himself.

Thinking on this, Annabelle smirked, *Not a great reputation, as he is known for grand parties and a new tootsie on his arm every weekend.*

Annabelle checked that her comportment was in order as she passed the mirrored doors to Carlton's office. It would never do to have him think she did not think highly of him.

"Yes, sir?" Annabelle asked sweetly, glancing at that smooth-shaven face and devil-may-care eyes of golden brown. Mainly she kept her eyes on the lips.

He licked them as though aware of her gaze and looked up—frantically waving her over. "I believe we are ready. Do you have the first half of the formula prepared?"

He knew she did, it had been ready for two weeks, but she dared not say so.

"Yes, Doctor."

"Well then, what are you standing here for? Hasten away and bring it forth!"

Annabelle hastened, with her long skirts hampering her ability, she raised them once out of his sight. She did have her reputation to keep, if only for him. The world already assumed she was there not for her ability, but for his pleasure.

It irked her all the more that the advances they made were all credited to him even though the last two were her ideas and completed, fully by half, through her own ingenuity and craft. True this one was nearly his idea, one inherited from his father. The desire to time travel was ever a goal, and the doctor could not give the dream up.

Returning with the chilled goo, she poured it into the awaiting shower-like enclosure engineer—making sure to cover the receptors.

The experiment had seemed to work when they sent a monkey; they hoped it had gone forward in time, at least it had departed for a minute and then returned in the same condition. Repeated tests came back with the same results. They had no way to really know where or when the test subject went, the chronometer it wore moved forward by twelve years. But the monkey appeared not to have aged, it truly was a puzzle. Cameras were sent, but the images returned white, blank, nothing. Though it ran the full 12 years, an amazing device in its own right.

Carlton stepped into the cubical, Annabelle assumed it was to ensure all was in order when to her horror, he shut the door and activated the device. The gel inch its way up the walls in electric blue glory. Something she found so mesmerizing in previous tests. As the color changed to turquoise, she knew the time was near. Yes, precisely as data predicted Dr. Carlton Dietrich vanished, their eyes locked mere moments before he winked out.

Annabelle was terrified, she waited until time had passed for when the monkey always returned, it was now ten minutes. She had called Dr. Scott and his assistant Dominic Schmitz. They worked on the same floor, developing programs for the PC's. Really it was their work which kept the company innovative—and lucrative.

Just as Dr. Scott was developing his rant against the young Doctor Dietrich, the man himself reappeared, collapsed upon the floor.

Annabelle fainted just being caught by Dominic.

Coming to, Annabelle recalled the vision which met her eyes mere moments before: The fair Adonis was horribly disfigured, his hair singed black, and his face melted and flame red. She turned and saw him being wheeled out on a brass cart made for carting away the dead. A soft cry escaped her lips as a medic came to help her.

"Sorry miss, din't mean ta scare ye. He still lives. Ye can visit him on the morrow."

Dominic nodded confirmation and Annabelle crumpled into his arms. Being that Carlton only hired the most beautiful people, neither minded the contact.

***

Weeks passed, and Dr. Carlton Dietrich was released to his residence. He refused to discuss the experiment but allowed Annabelle to sit with him as he recovered. Now that he was cleaned up, she saw the damage was not as bad as feared, but still bad enough.

All of his hair returned, though admittedly short. His eyes remained lovely, the left eye drooped a bit though. The still angry scar tissue pulled down as though he were made of melted wax. The tessellation of the grafts made a mockery of the ruined softness of his face as it continued down below the line of his gown, on the left side. Annabelle had learned from the nurse attending him that it ran the full length of his body to his pinky toe.

Learning to walk was tiresome, and he limped a bit. He had worn a pork pie hat and a black silken mask for the trip home. Once ensconced within his fortress, he feared the public eye and let all but two of his servants go. The cook and the gardener stayed; naturally, they took up the slack and did all the chores.

Annabelle was the only other person permitted in his presence, though she came to detest him all the more. His vanity had been ugly when he had been beautiful, now his rage removed any passion she had felt when looking upon his former glory.

But he still wanted to use her mind and talent. So her lab had been moved to his east wing. Daily she came to the great teak and brass gates which kept intruders out. It was an oddly beautiful set up, the showy gates had no connecting wall. Only lovely ornamental hedges and a plasma beam stood guarding the perimeter. Should any stray dog try to enter, it would be zapped upon contact. Hence no citizen dared even touch the hedges without the device being turned off, for fear of accidentally tripping and falling in. Children were warned to never even walk on the sidewalk, so fearful were their parents.

***

Two years passed, and Annabelle began to tire of her work. Being restricted to the east wing began wearing on her, so she wandered about looking at the vast wealth kept hidden and unloved. Salvador Dali's painting, the original mind you, hung upon the wall. Annabelle had to read the plaque to learn its name, "Persistence of Memory."

Oh, that is cruel, Annabelle thought. Surely Dr. Dietrich wishes to forget his past.

Continuing on into the main hall, she saw the familiar porcelain cat which greeted her each day when she arrived. The cat appeared to playfully bat at a metal butterfly which bobbed from a wire attached to the base of the sculpture. Picking it up, she saw that clockwork gears caused the butterfly to rotate and dance on its wire. She knew well enough that this was the case, but she was feeling daring and rash and wanted to violate the stern serenity of the home.

Emboldened by the view of the cat's inner workings, she audaciously made her way into the west wing of the home. The walls were papered in stripes of sage and a deep garnet; a rather garish combination, but it suited the brooding mood of the owner.

She peeked into rooms, viewing a conservatory with a white grand piano sitting lone and stark upon a teakwood stage. Such contrast! No parties had been held since she had come to work here at the estate. She felt cheated though she knew it was unreasonable. She had never liked the man, even when he was whole.

The doctor's own lab came next. Thankfully, he was not in. Annabelle found the library and longed to search the room for its treasures. But today she was merely exploring the inner reaches of the mansion.

Reaching the farthest room, she was delighted to find another lab, though it was more like another conservatory, for art rather than music. The glass wall allowed a view of the sunlight filtering through the leaves.

The sights beyond were equally enchanting as a water-wheel in the brook spun, powering—she assumed—the extra electricity the doctor burned up with all of his experiments. On a brass-plated counter sat an easel with a curious painting nearly complete. It appeared to be a wizard, yet something about him looked familiar. Yes . . . the eyes!

"Annabelle!" raged Carlton, "Who let you in here?"

"No one. I . . . "

"Precisely, I did not invite you, and yet here you are. Snooping among my things, trying to steal my secrets!" Carlton swiped at the counter knocking a sea gull's skull to the floor, it skittered to a stop at Annabelle's feet.

Annabelle decided it was time for a change, rashly she declared, "I came searching for you to let you know: I will be seeking employment elsewhere."

The sorrow in his eyes was instant and just as quickly replaced with cold, stony indifference, reminding her of tiger's eye, the gem stone, so richly golden and striped with brown, yet equally hard and cold.

"Very well, you may leave once you have completed the project you are working on. When it has been marketed . . . successfully, you will be free to pursue your own interests."

"But that is another year of work! Six months, if I am lucky." She knew it was in her contract that she could not leave under these circumstances, so though she wanted to rail against him. She shut her mouth. Gaining her composure, she stood as tall as her five-foot-four frame allowed and looked him in the eye.

The hurt and rage had returned to his eyes—warring within. She felt as if she viewed the inner clockworks of his soul, through his eyes. Looking at his still perfect mouth, she replied softly, "Forgive me, I am having a rough time getting past a tricky spot in my research."

Seeing that she was not leaving, Dr. Dietrich cleared his throat and replied, "Perhaps I should take a look. Would you care for tea before you return?"

It *was* tea time, and Annabelle *was* getting hungry, so she agreed. The cook, upon seeing the need, hastened back to the kitchen for another cup and more crumpets and biscuits.

Annabelle continued to scan the room, fully aware of Carlton's eyes upon her. In the window sat plants: ferns and ivy, a lovely collection of orchids, and brilliant passion flowers. The flowers were obviously a side experiment as the colors were far more vibrant than those found naturally. A crazy mobile hung from the ceiling sporting red string tied to brass tubing. Dragonflies were attached to the ends of each string, dragonflies which were, in fact, micro-robots. They flew about in a pre-programmed manner—ensuring that the string never tangled. It made her smile.

***

She did not see it, but her happy response caused Carlton's lips to twitch momentarily as well. How he admired her beauty! True she was short compared to his six-foot-two, but that made her seem all the more precious. He admired her spunk, never had he met a more brilliant mind, and yet he had never been able to tell her. He had hoped that the success of the time machine would have earned her respect. All it did was turn him into the monster she already believed him to be. He caressed her with his gaze; she had always worn her rich brown hair down in a low ponytail or hair clip. *When had she begun wearing it in that tight bun?* He frowned, it was not right; she deserved a better life than this.

Cook brought in the service and poured before bowing out.

"I would like to tell you what I saw that day," Carlton said huskily.

Annabelle looked up, green eyes wide, she could see his nervousness and yet a gleam of excitement too. "Really, you remember it?"

He smiled ruefully. "Yes, every whit. I was there twelve years, a future so far forward the people did not even have a history of our time frame at all. They counted it as the year 107 —meaning, one hundred and seven years since The Great Destruction. They did not know what the year had been before the catastrophe. They lived simply, in cinder-block homes. No clocks or time pieces, no electricity, nothing but the most primitive of devices really. Their leaders were called Wizards." Carlton nodded at the painting. "Yes, that was the Grand Wizard. He knew more than he let on, I challenged his authority and threatened his hold on the people. Suffice it to say he did not like me very well, but could not get rid of me as he had told the people that I would come and make their life better. He never told me how he knew, but it was in a book which he kept hidden in a chest." Carlton paused to dip his biscuit in his tea.

Annabelle scrutinized the wall behind him, it had a large fish tank filled with salt water creatures, brilliant fish swam like dancing flowers. A red octopus hid in a far corner as well as one which preferred to stay yellow, both of them were very striking against the blue and green backdrop and rocks. Beside the tank hung a grease board with cryptic notes written on it— *"She is a gatherer: moonlight, found wishes, moments of gratitude.* "And *"Live in the length of luxury."* Particularly troubling was, *"Knockout rats are now a reality."*

Shaking her head, she poured herself a second cup, and then replaced the rock candy swizzle stick into her tea, allowing it to melt before stirring gently. Cook knew her tastes and had included mint tea rather than regular. Removing the candy, she licked it before placing it once again on the platter. She cared not whether it was ladylike. She was nearing thirty and doubted she would marry, *why should I maintain propriety?* She smiled realizing she really was in a snarky mood. Looking up she blushed as she realized Carlton's eyes watched her intently.

"Please, continue. It's fascinating. So I assume you taught them basic skills like electricity, and plumbing and such crafts?"

"I did. Knowing that it would only be for twelve years, I tried to teach everything I thought they would need to thrive. Indeed as the final year approached they were living quite well. I must confess, I became close to a woman. We were married and blessed with two children. It had not been my original intent, but she captivated me." Carlton's eyes filled with tears. Annabelle became alarmed, she had never dealt with such emotions, her scientific mind was not used to such things!

Annabelle felt her own cogs whirring as she sought for an appropriate response, she blurted instead, "So you intend to return?"

"NO!" he cried out in anguish, slamming his tea cup down. "I cannot! The wizard was the one who harmed me, he set fire to my house killing my babes, and I do not know the fate of my wife, but I am sure she died from the severe burns. The medical advances I taught them were limited. The time machine deposits the subject within a cavern that sits above the village. The cavern is kept by the wizards, should any try to go there (to the future, I mean) they would be held captive. Before my departure-slash-return, The wizard Drayar told me he would ensure that all hated me for killing Shiana and our children."

The horror was too much for Annabelle, tears fell down her face. She placed her own tea cup down. *No wonder he was so upset, it was not solely the loss of his looks,* she reasoned. She placed a hand upon his. He held hers softly in return.

"I am so sorry, sir, for your loss."

"Please, we have known each other long enough, call me Carlton."

A curious thrill ran through Annabelle at the request. She nodded demurely and finished her meal.

They resumed their staid natures and went to Annabelle's lab to see what advice Carlton could give. Having changed into what would appear to be silken wet suits they then placed their goggles on for protection and entered the reaction chamber, where Annabelle was stumped on what to do to make the device work. It was supposed to be a hologram projector with the added function of transporting small objects from one place to another, using some of the same theories they had used for time travel. It was rather like an attache case only it could hold triple the amount. The projector showed the contents.

Carlton saw a deck of cards with the seven of diamonds face up and running shoes, a new fad that was gaining in popularity, even among the fairer sex. Also within, he viewed a seam ripper and a wrench. The content picture was displayed within a small notebook sized screen attached to the briefcase.

"So tell me where the difficulty lies."

Annabelle much preferred this interest in her work over the moody man she had been subject to over the past two and a half years; too she noted that she had not been paying attention. His grafts were working; his skin was nearly smooth and free from scarring. Yes, a bit still dripped to the side above his eye, but it seemed to add character. She realized he had asked a question.

"Sorry let me collect my thoughts." Annabelle blushed. "The difficulty is I can get them to appear to be within, but I cannot get them out. They are in reality still in the locations where they were when I aimed the recording device at them to capture them. But when I push the release button, like this, nothing happens. They are supposed to appear on the table when I push the appropriate button. There is one button for each item." She pointed at the twenty buttons on the lower edge of the box.

Carlton nodded. "Yes, that would make it seem like it were merely a vision box. What happens when you reach for them?" He reached his hand into the projection and pointed at the cards. Annabelle wanted to stop him, but he acted before she could say anything.

And then he had the cards in his hand.

"It appears to be working to me!" He grinned

Annabelle became animated as she saw the simplicity of her creation in work, "Wait, let me see if the cards are truly gone!"

She made her way to the far side of her lab, outside of the containment room.

***

Carlton enjoyed seeing her form in the protective gear he had designed a few years back. Normally she wore proper attire: skirts had inched up during his convalescence, so her ankles and a portion of her calves were revealed above her short boots. Her thin waist was cinched sweetly with a corset-like vest designed for outer wear, unlike the under clothing of yesteryear when such style was hidden from public view. She dispensed with bustled skirts—which were still in style—but she did not like them because they hindered her mobility in the lab.

But now she was truly liberated in the silky thin suit; she did not appear to realize how lovely she looked. It was one of the things he admired about Annabelle, her lack of self aware-ness.

Her voice sounded on the intercom, "Carlton, they are still here. Did you put them back?"

"No. Let me do it again."

***

Annabelle watched with awe as she watched the disembodied, wristless hand point at the cards. Making contact, the hand withdrew as though holding a deck of cards.

The two met half way between the two lab rooms, Carlton picked her up and swung her around in a circle as he crowed, "It's a replicator!"

Then Annabelle felt dazed as she responded to his kiss eagerly. The contact felt right and oh so solid. It had been a year and a half since she had stopped dating Dominic. And Carlton was superior in every way, she processed the data as she enjoyed the stimulus, ever scientific she could not help but compare and contrast.

Eventually, they broke away. "Annabelle, forgive the imposition. I realize I am a monster . . ." Carlton began, his own face coloring in shame.

Annabelle touched his face, it was soft if not entirely smooth. She was too short to kiss him unless he leaned down, so she merely stopped his mouth with her fingertips. "No, Carlton, I was wrong, you are no beast. You have pushed me to become the woman I am. Without you, I would never have created this device—even if I made it wrong." She smiled ruefully.

The smile tugged at Carlton's resolve, he smiled and searched her eyes for truth. "You do not find me hideous?"

She shook her head as he bent once more to place his lips on hers, those same lips which she had admired from afar.

Satisfied, Carlton pulled away. "Come with me. I have one thing I wish to try."

Leaving the lab in the flimsy though protective gear, Annabelle suddenly felt exposed, but Carlton was striding forth purposefully, so she doubled her steps to keep up. Making his way to his own lab, he went to a file cabinet and withdrew a stone, holding it out for her inspection. It was flat and had a mandala etched in brown upon its surface.

"What does the picture of the universe on a rock have to do with anything?" Voicing the thought she had meant to keep private, Annabelle softly smacked her face.

"I'll show you."

Carlton again strode the halls back to her lab. He recorded the stone pictogram with the specialized camera. Then entering the containment room, he replicated the stone several times. Annabelle was still puzzled but kept quiet, he appeared to know what he was about.

Taking his handful of stones back to his lab, Annabelle noted that he had another time machine behind a curtain which he revealed with a sweep.

Fearing he would go, she cried out, "Carlton, No!"

He smiled grimly and removed a female chimpanzee from another hidden location. Handing it the eight stones (on which he had hastily inscribed a numeral) he then placed the chimpanzee in the shower-like enclosure after having poured the goo as needed. Again the electric blue and turquoise, again the monkey disappeared. As before, it too stayed away the entire ten plus minutes. Only this time instead of returning as expected, to Annabelle and Carlton's surprise the Wizard appeared.

He was older than the painting portrayed, yet the eyes were still Carlton's.

Annabelle was confused. She reached for Carlton's hand as the man stood in his rough woven robes, yellowed with age or simply never having been white—she could not tell.

"Carl," he said. "What took you so long? Ah, never mind. I do believe your efforts have done the trick. That chimp was right clever and handed me the stones. I placed them as per your instructions. And, Carl I wish to apologize for the . . . erm, distrust I placed in you. You may be happy to know that the destruction of your wife and bairns was mere illusion. It was necessary to make you leave and complete your objectives. They are grown and are soon to set off on their own journeys. She is at peace, all has been explained."

He then bowed to Annabelle. "Our Lady of the New Dawn, you honor me with your presence." With that, he flipped the switch and departed.

Carlton sobbed but held Annabelle close. She was completely lost but waited for his grief or joy to ease. *Will he leave knowing his wife lives? And what was with the Lady of the New Dawn reference?* Her mind once again whirred in clockwork precision and yet she could see no reason. So she waited.

He kissed her once, gently cupping her face. She feared it was the last kiss and waited to hear his announcement of departure.

"We did it!" His face beamed, and his eyes shone with such fervor.

"Annabelle you did it, for this you will be revered as *She who saved the few.* Those few willing to seek protection when The Great Destruction strikes."

Carlton went on to explain that the replicator allowed him to create portals to various locations around their region. "In the future that I visited only that one location was known to have survived, but now Wizard Drayar has let me know that more have been saved."

"Then why not send more?" Annabelle asked.

Carlton sighed. "I did not tell you the entire truth. I did read the Books of Dietrich, their history books. Book one was written by me, books two and three by my son and then his son. Yes, Drayar is a descendant. I could not get him to reveal how many generations. But the books reveal that the innovations which scientists released years ago evolved and became destructive to nature. The nano bots which were designed to eat waste and pollution. They did not die out as expected; they became ravenous and ate up entire continents. Most of the America's were destroyed—Africa, Asia, not a plant left. Only the highest and coldest reaches were left untouched. Then I assume the nano bots had nothing left to consume and died out. Only those pockets of safety created by Carlton Dietrich the third were able to survive.

"In the future that I visited, the plants had made their way below the mountain's high reaches. With stored seeds the survivors were able to begin anew. They had been at it only seventy years as they had stayed within the shelters the first thirty-seven. Still, I was able to walk, in one day, to the edge and see the wastelands, so dry and bereft. At first, I believed it was bomb blasted. Never would I have thought such little creations could wreak such havoc. So no, the circle of safety cannot be extended much further. Since the people in the place I visited cannot travel very far due to lack of life giving plants. In the book which I am about to write, I will instruct them to travel in eight opposing directions and place the portals. But they must be within caves. And they must be done in that time frame, not ours. The original, this one which I made," he held up the stone with the mandala scribed upon it.

"This one will be handed down and taken to the cave by the ancestor of Drayor. In the days of some future descendant, the time machines I will have built will transport those who believe in the predicted future to the safety of the caves. They will need to be stocked and supplied with seeds and food and supplies necessary for life and comfort. Few will believe the ramblings of a recluse and his assistant. Fewer still will believe their posterity."

Annabelle finally understood. She was to be the progenitor of many of those saved. Her discovery would save mankind. Looking up into those golden-striped eyes, she saw love.

He was to be her universe, together they would achieve harmony and peace. His innermost secrets were revealed, and she marveled at the complex beauty of his mind and soul.

"Okay," she replied as though he had proposed. Then acting as if he had, he took her in his arms and kissed her heartily once more.

Neither one minded the impropriety.

Chapter 16

Delicacies

Alas, all good things come to an end, as I well know. I had a unique visitor chance by only last week. I have nearly compiled this book of tales, but this story was so fascinating I could not help but add it to my collection.

I chuckle at my own thoughts as I consider this a love story of a whole other fabric and meaning. Be that as it may, my visitor was a Troll who served the Troll King. He came up from the depths to enter my Emporium, in search of a particular treasure. Amazingly he found it too. The story is about the Troll King, and I will take my guest's word as true. Sadly, when I inquired as to how he himself came to know about this little escapade, the Troll coughed up a bit of green slobbery goo and replied, "Not your business to know. Besides you old son-of-a-trickster, I have paid you with one story. I will leave out the front, I am feeling a bit hungry myself."

And with that he walked out of the shop as the sun settled. Oddly, I noted he had not donned a glamour, or disguise. I pity the Humans still on the streets.

The Troll King slurped, unconcerned with his appearance. Slobbering was a natural state for Trolls and a mere thought triggered the juices flowing. Smell can cause great ribbons to stream. Ever a favored snack was Fairy as they are so sweet and delightful. Alas, he was barred from such treats. As he sat, there in his caged cave, he thought back to when he was younger and free. A tortuous exercise to be sure, but dinner would be served soon and it would satisfy, if not entirely please.

His most delightful delicacy had chanced upon him once when he had used a glamour to disguise his natural green hued skin and minimize his height and girth. Seven feet tall was just too large to blend in. In his disguise, wrought by magic, he appeared to be a six-foot-five football player with a wide but handsome face.

The year as had among Humans was 1970. He was in Sacramento.

The smell of all the Human flesh was so tantalizing, yet he had snacked before he set out and truly, he did enjoy a well cooked meal. Tony's Bar and Grill served an all you can eat steak bonanza. That is if you can eat the first 32 ounce steak and potato you get a second one for free. Well he could and had done so on many an occasion, usually in the company of fellow Trolls. But tonight he was on his own.

As he finished the second steak, a scent wafted into the room. Sending the drool down to soak his shirt. Hastily he slurped it back as this was one scent he would not give up on.

There she was, a cute blonde with her waist length hair done up in crinkly waves, wafting her scent in every direction. She was on the prowl Olkin could tell. Her eyes scanned the room, even as she acted casual, drink in hand, making eye contact, and swiftly dismissing her target.

He made eye contact. It was electric, she grinned and made her way to him. They danced, each inhaling often, and laughing when they caught the other. He relished in her softness, she felt so delicate beneath his hands. She allowed his touch so he hungrily caressed her body as they swayed to the music. She encouraged him to take the lead.

"It's getting a little stuffy in here; I am going to take a breather. Care to join me?" he asked.

"Not at all," she replied, lifting her hair as if to cool her neck.

The pair walked out leaving many a male prospects eyes saddened, as her scent had enticed them as well. For she was indeed a Vampire. Olkin had only heard of their allure and having finally chanced upon one he was not about to lose her.

As he guided her towards a shadowed alley, he felt her muscles tighten and her scent increased. He knew that the scent was meant to slow down Humans, but for him it merely increased his hunger. Turning towards her as she designed, he said, "You smell so delightful I could just eat you up."

She grinned revealing fangs and replied, "I was just about to say the same."

She rushed and Olkin enjoyed the shock as he moved faster than any Human prey she had ever encountered. The juice filled his mouth and he sated his desire, consuming every last bite. Never had a meal been so satisfying!

***

The only thing to be found in the morning was her faded jeans and a few shreds of her shirt as well as the beads she wore attractively around her head. No blood, no crime scene. The cook simply picked the clothes up with a tsking noise and threw them in the dumpster.

***

Olkin sighed as half a beef was carried in for his dinner. Raw and juicy, lovely, but never so wonderful as that sweet bloodless Vampire in 1970.

Chapter 17

Familiars

My final offering for this compilation of cherished tales is one that I had been told beforehand is entirely fictional. Though I have my doubts. A witcher woman from the early 1800's chanced to enter my shop one dreary afternoon. She entered to get out of the rain, but once inside she could not help but browse a bit. She ended up purchasing several medical books as well as a few mortar and pestle sets.

Again I have my doubts, but the woman seemed to startle when she noticed the portal, she then asked me to allow her through. She seemed to believe it would be a shortcut home. But who am I to say if it was true or not?

I sat transfixed as she wove her masterful spell. I could see plainly why she accepted the title of witch even though no such enchantress exists.

As for me, I would dearly love to use the portal to take me home. But where is home anyway?

Millicent was late. Not unusual for her, she never learned to tell time so looking at the clock was no help. Of course, when Fianna called her children to dinner, Millie knew she ought to be leaving.

Millie was friends with Eleanor; at seventeen they were considered adult. Had Millicent lived in town her mother would have insisted on her having an escort. But they were country folk, and Millie knew her way home in the dark.

Not that it was dark just yet. It was six o'clock and the sun was only hidden by the close growing trees. Making her way she hummed the new tune Eleanor's brother had been teaching the family before dinner. Gerard was two years older and seemed so wise to Millie. She had admired him since she was a toddler. Not that she ever admitted such, not even to Eleanor. His dark brown hair which curled past his ears and warm golden flecked green eyes never ceased to pull her gaze.

He had been taking classes at the castle proper. At the Wizard Academy actually, though he was not yet accepted as an apprentice. It was a start and something she knew he had dreamed of since Millie had started paying attention to his fantastical tales.

Entering the thickest part of the woods, where the trees reached out like a canopy, blocking the light over the track, Millie thought about Gerard's most recent tales.

True she had heard the likes before, but considering where he worked she began to believe they may be true.

"Master Transom taught that in order to transform the

very first time, familiars need a powerful stimulus." Gerard said, awe tinged his baritone voice.

Little golden-haired Caryn quickly interrupted, "What is stimulus?"

Gerard poked his littlest sister and said, "Motivation, desire." His eyes chanced on Millicent's warm brown eyes when he said 'desire' causing her face to warm. Dropping her eyes, and hiding her face in her near auburn curls, she missed his slight smile.

"Be that as it may, he taught that the last familiar in this region was Master Tyndale of Greenwood." This time he looked at Millie directly as all gasped. With a chuckle he continued, seeing the question on everyone's faces. "I know! I was just as surprised myself, Master Josiah Tyndale was Millie's own great grandfather. And you have never heard such tales Millie?" He kept his eyes upon her.

Millie shrugged, "I heard a few tales as a young girl, but stopped believing as I grew. Modern girls do not believe such fantasy…at least I didn't *think* we did."

Gerard smiled broadly now, his straight white teeth catching the light shining in the window. "Well, he truly could transform into an owl, and having become attached to his sweetheart, Miranda, she was the only female admitted to the Academy in ages. Now we know why she is called the Witch of Greenwood."

Perhaps such thoughts were not best to ponder as one trampled through the woods at dusk. Millie thought she heard a sound, more like a scuffle. *Could be a startled deer.* She continued on past the tree marking the midway point in the darkest patch of Greenwood Forest.

Further tales said that the ancient tree, which stood as

sentinel, was in very deed the center of the forest and parent to all the rest, having been planted in a vast field by a traveling wizard in ages past. It was said to be sentient, indeed it could help or hinder a traveler's passage. Millie had never seen it do a blessed thing. But tonight it seemed to loom ever so ominously, the breeze stirred it's branches. She stopped, and heard unmistakable footfalls and a low curse.

Fear gripped her, it was still one half mile to the other side of the woods and her home another quarter mile from the edge. Who would be in the woods anyway? Her mind ran several directions at once. She determined that climbing the tree might be her best bet, she could never out run a man. But, perhaps she could get to a high limb; one too thin to support a man's weight.

Fly

Millie heard the thought as though it had been shouted, and yet she knew it was in her head.

Hastily she ran and heard a snicker which caused her to turn, *Never turn!* she chided, as fear froze her movement.

Three men rounded her, she heard a fourth on the other side of the tree. Loudly snapping branches with never a care now.

She felt him before he spoke, he caressed her cheek with a soft, smooth hand. Funny how details are noticed at times like these. Millicent couldn't help but think how odd it was for a ruffian, or woodsman to have such a delicate touch.

"A wee bit late for a lass to be out on her own. What?" he asked.

Millie had no answer.

Fly! Fly now!

Millie desperately wished she could.

The men before her were not as smooth as the man now holding her wrist, even in the gloom she could see they were unclean, an odor wafting her way confirmed what her eyes saw.

"Well, sir, is she the one!" asked a stooped man as he eyed her hungrily.

"Aye, she is the very one I sought." He reached to his pocket, Millie assumed for a rope.

Her dread increased as she feared no escape, with a screech she flapped her arms with force, anger and fear. To her amazement she was airborne and soon above the forest altogether.

Yes!

What have I done?

That which you were born to do

Millie hated obfuscation, angrily she flapped harder rising to a warm, soft air current. With joy she hovered and spied the four mischief makers.

What about them? Will they not cause harm to my family?

Come to me, and we will seek help.

Millie was confused, she had assumed that it was perhaps the ancient tree speaking to her. She spied the tree and landed in the highest branches, out of sight of those below.

How can you help?

Mirth was conveyed, and more shocking, a tender love. * Millie 'tis I, Gerard. I followed, feeling anxious about your safety. Please come to me, to the north—near the stream. *

Silently she winged her way. There in the dark, clearly seen with her owlish eyes, Millie saw he whom she loved, his arm outstretched, she landed with some force. He staggered a bit as he whistled.

"Such a beauty. Millie you are a Snow Owl just like your great grandfather!"

Millie reverted at will to her own form, and then turned hastily away as she found she was naked. Gerard draped his cloak about her shoulders.

"Sorry, that part was not in the lesson."

Millie was shocked at all which had transpired. But first she wanted to ensure her reality.

"Does this mean we are bonded?"

Gerard warmed at the question, she could see his pulse quicken in his now exposed throat. "Aye, surely we have always been bonded."

With joy she kissed him, not mindful of her state. He, of course, had not a care at all though her state was certainly on his mind.

Momentarily they ceased their ardent response and returned to the task at hand. Having deemed her flight would be swifter, she took to the air as he ran towards her home to warn her family.

The witcher woman in my Arcadium stopped her tale there as she said she had pressing matters to attend. But she assured me the family was warned and the ruffians captured by the castle's roving guards. And, of course, she affirmed the tale had a happily ever after ending.

As for me, the gatekeeper, or grand Portal Master, if you will, I wait upon news of and from my father. My cousin did return and has informed me that my father has not been seen by anyone at all for decades. He is locked up within a room down the eastern hall of the Void.

He is searching for answers, as are we all.

I pray he finds them, and that I am part of the answer. But to whom does a denizen of the deep pray? And at what price?

I feel as if I have paid many times over for the service I have rendered. I long for freedom, for truth and answers.

Yes, answers to those deep questions: who am I, and where do I belong? I think knowing these things will give me greater direction and purpose. I feel a need growing within, a sense that something of great import is soon to sweep me away. Silly I know to think a dusty old Goblin too big to fit in a burrow would be of worth to the goings-on in the world. Yes, mere fantasies and hopes.

But for now, I am The Gatekeeper: Collector of Tales.

I thank you for spending this time with me.

~ Volé